3-98

HER WILD
AMERICAN
SELF

HER WILD

AMERICAN
SELF

SHORT STORIES BY
M. EVELINA GALANG

COFFEE HOUSE PRESS :: MINNEAPOLIS

The following stories have appeared or are forthcoming in slightly different form in the following publications: "Our Fathers" in *Riksha*, and *Special Edition Press*; "Rose Colored" in *Amerasia Journal*, and *New Voices*; "Talk to Me, Milagros" in *The Crescent Review*; and "The Look-Alike Women," "Lessons You Never Learned Back Home," and "Mix Like Stir Fry" in *Quarterly West*; "Filming Sausage" in *American Short Fiction*, and "Her Wild American Self" in *Calyx*.

Cover Illustration/Design by Patsy Welch

Back cover photograph by Kate Kronick

Book design by Jinger Peissig

This project has been made possible through a major grant from the Star Tribune/ Cowles Media Company. Additional support has been provided by the Minnesota State Arts Board, through an appropriation by the Minnesota State Legislature; the National Endowment for the Arts; the Lila Wallace-Reader's Digest Fund; The McKnight Foundation; Lannan Foundation; Jerome Foundation; Target Stores, Dayton's, and Mervyn's by the Dayton Hudson Foundation; General Mills Foundation; St. Paul Companies; Honeywell Foundation; Beverly J. and John A. Rollwagen Fund of The Minneapolis Foundation; Prudential Foundation; and The Andrew W. Mellon Foundation.

Coffee House Press books are available to the trade through our primary distributor, Consortium Book Sales & Distribution, 1045 Westgate Drive, Saint Paul, MN 55114. For personal orders, catalogs or other information, write to:
Coffee House Press
27 North Fourth Street, Suite 400
Minneapolis, MN 55401

ISBN 1-56689-040-3

10   9   8   7   6   5   4   3   2   1

contents

AUTHOR'S ACKNOWLEDGMENTS

I'd like to thank my parents, Miguel and Gloria Galang, for teaching me all those lessons—especially the ones on perseverance, determination, and preservation—preservation of self, family and community. You taught me how to make a good life despite the American Dream.

Thank you too, Judith Kitchen and Stan Rubin—adopted parents of mine —who stole me from the film industry and planted me deep into the thing I love most—the reading and writing of stories.

I'd also like to thank my teachers: Lorrie Moore, Kelly Cherry, Steven Heller, Marjorie Sandor, Leslee Becker, John Clark Pratt, Elsa Santos, John Calderazzo, and David Milofsky. Special thanks to Steven Schwartz, my advisor, for teaching me how to dig up all that material and pointing me in the direction of illumination rather than illustration.

Thanks to my families in the film industry: Sedelmaier, Chicago Story, Dix and Associates, Ed, and Komenich for supporting me all those years, and every single summer, making this transition a sweet one.

I'd like to thank Jody Rambo Buckman, Kristin Benson Pederson, Wendy Rawlings, Christina Robertson, Leslie Patten, and Susan Abattista. Your voices will always be with me.

Thank you, Chris Erickson. You were right.

Special thanks to Elaine Dawson at Old Dominion University—for all those drafts and rewrites. Thank you, Tessa Garcia for the use of your Locin family photo.

Lastly, thank you to all the women, girls, and babies in the Galang and Lopez-Tan households—for your stories, your inspiration, and most of all for your dreaming.

*For my parents Mike and Glo—
adventurous travellers, risk takers
and fabulous storytellers.*

THE LOOK-ALIKE WOMEN

Because you are all beautiful—but in different ways. Your skin, yellow and light as the moon; and other times, the color of the earth, of clay from the red rocks, from the mountain; or baked goldenbrown like the crust of honey bread.

Because you have dark hair, fine like the silk from milkweed, or coarse like hemp and black like a sleeping universe, so black it shines blue. Your hair melts in the wind, strays from the face. A face that's sometimes round like mother-of-pearl from the bottom of the sea or angular like the rocks at the edge of that same ocean.

Because you are all exotic. Sensual and mysterious as red silk kimonos. Passionate like volcanoes, Mount Fuji and Pinatubo. Sexy like the girls who danced in clubs along Olongapo. Fierce like Miss Saigon. Crafty like Mata Hari. Obedient like the Geisha girls from old Japan or the mail order brides, the ones in the glossy catalogues. Because you bear children well and please your husbands—always your husbands first.

Because you are ladies. Because you've been raised to wait for the man. Wait for him. He will ask you. He will guide you. Protect you. Comfort you. Provide you with everything—everything except the cooking and the cleaning and the ironing and the children and the bookkeeping and the house and the rest.

Because you are smart, all smart. Book-smart, doctors, lawyers, chemists. Sense-smart wives and daughters. Some of you follow your intuition; some of you follow the rules learned in books, equations of the mind. And still there are those of you who follow the lessons you've learned from your mothers. Other wise women. Other sisters. Others.

Because you know the finer arts. Because you are a dancer, a violinist, a pianist, a poet, a fabulous cook, a seamstress of fine needlework, a painter, a singer, a movie star, the center of attention.

Because you are so well-behaved, never speaking out of turn. Never speaking up. Subservient. Obedient. Quiet. Because no one sees you hiding away in the library, surrounded by your stacks of books, or working late at the lab, or typing madly at your computer during all hours of the night, or painting walls inside your house, or shaving wood and sanding old tables and vanities. Because no one sees you carrying stones for your garden, the chairs for the dining room, the sofa. They call you orchid, silk rose, golden butterfly. Because no one bothers to look when you are standing up. When you're speaking out. Because when they do, you are an anomaly. One of a kind. Wave maker.

Because "different" is not looked upon endearingly. Because friends are hard to find. To keep. Because it's easier to just let them believe what they want to believe. Because even though you look more Chinese than your sister Edna, who looks Spanish like your grandmother, they all say, "I can hardly tell you two apart." Because there seem to be no lines, no walls, between the Japanese, Vietnamese, Koreans, Chinese and the Filipina, even you have come to believe you are no different than the rest. The look-alike women, the beautiful women. The women of the Orient.

ROSE COLORED

I'm standing at the corner of Washington and LaSalle, trying to keep my feet still upon the sidewalk, but people rushing past sway me right, then left. Bump me. Push me. Toss me dirty looks. I'm waiting for the light to change.

Next to me stands a woman, gathering glances from all around her. She stands oblivious to her admirers. I wonder how she can't see them. People who stare make me nervous. When I sense someone watching, I look to my shoes, click my heels, make myself disappear. But she doesn't seem to care. She's nearly six feet tall and has long brown hair tinged with red, straight and free as a hula skirt. Her cheek bones are high, square and smooth. And her eyes are black almonds. She looks more Asian than white, though her skin is still paler than the brown of my own. She stands up against the wind, the current of people and the sun's glare as it bounces from a sea of chrome bumpers. When a cab slows next to the curb, she is the only one who waves it away. Other people scramble to the cab like rats to a sewer hole. I wonder how she came to be so strong, my beautiful cousin Mina.

"Let's grab the El. It's a few blocks away," she tells me. "Come on, Rose."

I follow her, as I have always followed her. When we were small, I would spend summers at Mina's house in Connecticut.

Then, I'd follow her around the neighborhood, through fields and creeks. Mina always knew where the boys kept their secret hide-outs. And the boys would always pretend to hate her, but I could see then what I see now, Mina is beautiful. Nobody hates Mina. "Wait for me!" I shout. I feel the curls in my hair sagging with the heat. I look up. She's floating across traffic, gliding between cars and I'm stuck at the median. "Wait!" I call out again. I drag my suitcase on wheels and it slips between my legs. "I can't go that fast." But she is already on the other side of the street, waving past taxis, distracting pedestrians. And I feel so short and ugly.

We take the elevated train to Mina's neighborhood. On the way there, we pass forgotten chimneys, weathered back porches, clotheslines weeping with socks and shirts. In the distance there is a curtain of haze behind which lies the Chicago skyline. This is what Mina shows me. She points: "See over there? The John Hancock Building and the Sears Tower." What I see are the factories, paint chipping from its brick and yet brightly decorated by gang graffiti. What I see are telephone poles and pigeons, going on forever like water in an ocean. Each time the train grinds to a stop, heat rises from under the tracks, suffocating breath and sound. Unbearable.

But all I say to Mina is, "Wow, that's amazing." I'm not sure what I'm looking for. Maybe mountains and snow caps, maybe evergreen trees.

A man stands next to our seat, carrying a leather attaché. His body is encased in a starched white shirt and business suit. He wears a power tie—the yellow kind with navy pin-point polka-dots. He has a face that is smooth and pretty. I look up to him and watch a dimple peel across his cheek. Across from us, another man stares. He is about fifty years old. And even though it's one hundred and some degrees he wears a flannel shirt, a parka and a woolen hat. His face is unshaven and weathered like a prune. His bottom lip curls in and out as he breathes. He sits like bananas in garbage, like bodies gone stale. He's scary and I can feel my shoulders rising as I watch him watch us.

"Excuse me," says the young executive beside us. I turn my face up to him, push the sleeve from my wrist, ready to give him the time of day when he says, "Are you women from China?" Mina ignores him. "Miss," he repeats, "do you speak English?"

Mina slowly turns to the man, her hair falling away from her shoulder, eyes widening as she examines him. "No," she says, "sorry to say, I don't. Do you Rose?"

I smile at the man in slight embarrassment. "Mina —"

"Are you from China?" he asks.

"Does it matter?" she wants to know. Mina clenches her jaw, her face drawn and irritated red.

"Vietnam?" he persists. "I'm sorry, it's just that you're both so beautiful. You remind me of a Chinese woman I used to love."

"Oh please!" Mina laughs. The train lurches forward. She grabs my arm.

"Come on, Ling-Rose-Lee, this is our stop."

There are trees down this street, big and old. A narrow strip of grass lines the sidewalk. The homes, a series of dingy brick bungalows accented occasionally by newly fixed houses, are close together. I find this, like the crowds on the street and the air on the train, suffocating. People sit on their front steps. Some wave to Mina. Some say hello. There are cats everywhere, alley cats hidden behind bushes, under cars, between garbage cans. Even they come out of hiding, brush past her leg, make note of Mina as she passes.

In Louisville, I have a house set in the middle of grass. The driveway is long and the house lies hidden among the trees. I like the privacy. I like not having people on top of me, knowing my business, asking me questions. Snooping. I don't even know my closest neighbors who live almost a mile away from me, though someone once told me they were a newly wed couple, both surgeons. When Eddy and I marry this summer, he'll move into my house. It will be our house, even though he's asked me to sell it. "I want a place of our own," he'd said. It took a while, but I won and he's moving in with me.

"What do Uncle and Auntie say about you living here?"

"They sent me money to put bars on my windows," Mina says. "They'll get over it."

She calls out to the neighborhood kids, "Hey! What's up?"

A gathering of children rush past us on bikes and big wheels. "*Hola* Mina!" some cry. "Hello *Señorita*!"

A woman, big and doughy, rakes a patch of dirt. She wears a flowered muumuu, sun hat and rubber thongs. "How are you, Anna?" Mina calls out.

Anna looks up and flashes us a toothless smile. "Ah," she says, "Mina." Her hands gesture for my cousin, who puts her willowy arms about Anna's shoulders. "Mina, Mina, Mina," she chants.

"Anna, I want you to meet my cousin Rose." Mina points to me.

"Hello," I say, extending my hand, "I'm Rose *Al-jan-dro*." Anna grabs my hand and pulls me into her bosom. With her arms she cradles me, rocking me and cooing.

"*Al-jan-dro?*" Mina says. "What's that? *Ala-hhhhhan-dro*. It's our name, show some respect, would you?"

"What's she doing?" I ask.

"This is Anna's way of welcoming you. She and her son Nicholas are from Poland and she doesn't speak so much English, so she does body talk." Mina leans into the two of us, rubbing Anna's thick arm. "Where's Nicky?" Mina asks.

"School," Anna says.

"Nicholas goes to a special school for challenged young adults," Mina tells me.

I make an attempt to break free from Anna's embrace. Then she wraps her hands about the edges of my face, smiling and uttering incomprehensible gibberish, making me feel trapped and uneasy.

"Yes, she is very lovely, Anna, even if she can't pronounce her own name." Mina pats the top of my head. "Anna says you gotta come to dinner one night—she'll cook a good Polish meal." Anna squeezes my cheeks tight like a wet rag for rinsing.

"That's nice, Mina," I tell her. "Now make her let go. Make her stop."

*

The next day, Mina wakes early. I feel her silent movements. And I imagine her going through her morning routine as if it were a dance. Sliding from her bed to the shower, gliding like a stream of water into the kitchen and up the stairs.

When I wake she is still dressed in leotards that are as pink and worn as an old dancer. Her expression is calm, her body relaxed. She sits at the kitchen table, one leg wrapped around her body, twisted and somehow comfortable as a house cat.

"I thought I heard you dancing," I tell her. "What time did you get up?"

"Five."

"And you're still in your leotards?" I pour myself a cup of coffee. "You're lucky. Even when I have time to work-out in the morning, I've got to get going right away. In fact, most days I'm too busy to think about anything but work."

"Warm-ups and work-outs are part of my job, Rose. It's what dancers do. Not to mention that I have a two-hour dance class with the company at nine." She stares at me.

"I guess I'm just used to thinking of work as spread sheets and numbers and navy blue suits." She stares. "Secretaries and phone messages on little pink slips."

"I gotta run, lady banker," Mina says. She walks out of the kitchen and calling back to me adds, "Wanna come?"

*

The taxi smells of people's bodies, overworked, under-bathed, food-drenched bodies. There is a constant garble of frequencies and voices resonating in the cab. Inside this coach everything is hot and muggy and I am near nausea.

"Hubbard and Orleans," Mina tells the driver.

"Where are you from?" asks the cabby.

"Chicago," answers Mina. "Cousin Rose hails from Ohio."

"I mean —" the driver says, speaking with a foreign accent I don't recognize.

"Yeah, yeah, yeah, I know. The Philippines. Rose's parents and my dad are from the Philippines. My mom is second generation Irish—she's from Queens."

I look into his rear view mirror. It's twice the size of the regular one, stretching into the back seat, magnifying our every feature. My face looks broad and pulled like taffy. My cheeks seem to spread across the entire cab. The mirror pulls my eyes to the corners of my forehead, slits my eyes in half and pushes my nose flat against my face. I look so alien.

"So, do you have a steady job yet?" I ask.

"I have a job, Rose, I dance."

You dance, I think, laughing. That's a job? A job is where a person goes to make money. Finds ways to pay the rent and buy the things you need to eat, to wear, to pay electric bills. A job is work, not dancing. I work. I enter that bank every day and sit at my terminal sometimes for ten hours. That's a job. I'm still laughing, but Mina stares at me and remains silent and then I say, "No, I mean, that's a great job, Mina. Dancing. Great."

*

Five rows of dancers stand four abreast. I watch through a glass plate from the floor above. Her body is long and boy-like. Her legs seem to flow into her thighs and lose themselves somewhere in the torso. From this distance, she seems frail. But then the music starts.

She raises her arms in unison with the class and I feel energy circling the room like wind pushing through an Indian summer. Her heels touch one another and her toes point in opposite directions. Slowly she bends her knees and though her body moves toward the ground, her head is up, her chest pushes out into spaces around her. Mina's arms are taut with power and she appears to be the tallest one in the class. There's strength in this one solitary move, there's tension pushing her down, pulling her up. When multiplied by five rows of dancers, four abreast, this one plié is breathtaking.

The room shines with the dancers' energy. Their faces light spaces between them. I think about my fluorescent office. How I pass the body of secretaries as I move into my own space. How I place my body at the terminal and plunge into a trance of numbers and figures and faceless accounts. I zone out of myself and fill in the data, feeding my computer, waiting for the end of the day when I will spend my time dreaming and planning the vacation of a lifetime. My honeymoon. My wedding.

*

During the next few days, I barely see Mina. This morning she leaves for class as I sit at a window that looks out the side of the house. I can see into Anna's sitting room—a stuffed chair, an old table, a vase full of flowers. I'm writing to Eddy: *"Sometimes we have dinner, or she goes to rehearsals with her dance company. On weekends she dances at a club. Mina's a go-go dancer. Can you believe that?"*

As I write I feel as though someone is watching me. I look about the house. Mina has little figurines scattered on various tables and counters, little Filipino folk dancers caught in the midst of movement, their eyes shining full of life—of glass.

Soon, I hear pounding and then the low moan of a voice. I ignore it. The sound persists, grows stronger and louder. I look up out the window. I scream.

There's a man in the window. His head is narrow while his eyes seem to jut from the frame of his face. His nose is large and crooked, protrudes like a beak on an eagle. Nothing seems to fit his tiny head. His cheeks are pocked with disease. His lips pucker into a solitary "o." He waves at me, pounding the windows and spitting out some message. He stops talking and stares at me. His head leans left, ready to fall like an apple from a tree. Embarrassed, I jump from my seat and hide in the safety of

Mina's windowless bathroom. Sitting on the toilet, still shaking, I finish the letter to Eddy. I tell him how much I hate the city—the dangerous city—the city where there is no normality or privacy or even space to write in peace.

*

That night, Mina comes home early. When I tell her about the incident with the scary man, she laughs. "That was Nicky," she says. "He was probably just saying hi."

"That's Nicky? What's wrong with him?"

"An illness that struck him suddenly a couple years ago left him paralyzed and shriveled up his body. But his mind is strong."

"He scared me to death."

"Look, I'll make you dinner tonight. Relax. Nicky's harmless." She pulls pans out of the cupboard. "Usually I'm too busy to cook in the middle of the week, but our director's got the flu, so . . ." She makes chicken *adobo*, *pansit* and rice.

"Where'd you learn to cook this stuff?" I ask.

"*Lola*. Everyone says I cook like *Lola*."

When we were young our parents would take us to these Filipino picnics. There was always folk dancing and bad electric guitars and singing. This always happened in a public park and we kids were devastated by this display of ethnicity.

Personally, I've always tried to stay away from ethnic any-thing—things that make me different than the rest. I don't like to stand out in the crowd. I don't like to be noticed. Maybe it had to do with coming to Louisville Elementary in fifth grade. By then everyone had their own clique—and all those cliques used to sur-round me and taunt me with fake Japanese words. They'd take their fingers and pull at the corners of their eyes. They'd shuffle around me pressing their knees and their palms together, calling me a Chink.

"Remember that one white lady who used to sing songs in *Tagalog*?" I ask.

"Yeah—she was married to Bernie Sol."

"Talk about trying too hard."

"I suppose she was trying to fit in," Mina says. "Nothing wrong with that." She crushes garlic under a heavy silver blade. "What about those games with all the kids?"

There was the piñata and that game with the bean bag. You'd stand around in circles kicking the bag up into the air to other players. "God," I say, "it was so queer."

"I don't know." She heats a huge pan on the stove, douses it in oil, tosses in the garlic. "I think we thought it was queer—but really it was okay—fun."

"We hated those dances, Mina. We hated practicing."

The dance is about a princess and slave boy who meet while crossing the river. Mina struts across the kitchen with her head up. She holds her hand out to an imaginary servant. She dips her foot into the river, a hallway between the kitchen and the dining room. "It's a beautiful dance."

Mina's hips sway and her bare feet slip across her floor. Hands slap against her thighs in an attempt to imitate the rhythm of the bamboo poles. It's clear to me that the only reason she loved that dance was because she always danced the princess. I, on the other hand was cast the part of the handmaid, a servant bamboo clapper.

"I don't eat much rice. Or soy sauce," I tell her.

"I miss this stuff. I get homesick and then I cook."

"Eddy and I eat out a lot."

I lean back in my chair and gaze at candle wax dripping onto the table, sip a glass of wine and sigh. Vinegar, garlic, soy sauce and pepper flavor my breath with memories long forgotten.

As a child, I remember running around the dining room table where plates of chicken and noodles, and whole pigs roasted over makeshift spits, sat among salads and fruits, rich desserts and breads. My *Lola* and *Lolo's* house was always filled with food and family and really bad jokes. I always wanted a big family like my grandparents, but Eddy has convinced me that having five or six kids would not be prudent—"Not with our economy being the way it is, Rose," he'd said.

She pours grains of rice into a huge pot and fills that with water. She plunges her hand into the pan, cleaning the flour off the rice. "You know, my parents are always on my back. They want me to marry and settle down. 'Why can't you be like Rose?' They want to know. 'She's practical'."

"They're just getting old. They probably want grandkids."

"Well, I've told them to live vicariously through your mom and dad. I'm not ready."

"Who says I am?" I brush the tablecloth with my hand, dusting off bits of stale rice. "If I was like you, I'd have moved to New York," I say.

"Broadway?" She asks.

I nod. "But it's time. Settling down is what I'm supposed to do. Look at my hips—they're ready to deliver."

When we were little girls I used to sit in my room making up plays, writing out parts for us. I'd show her the scripts, and together we'd create these family performances. Of course, she always got the role of the girl, I was either the guy or the evil witch or mad scientist, the one who always tried to get the girl. I liked that part. I liked being up on stage and pretending, trying to triumph over the silly princess or the trusting red-hooded child. Back then, I wanted to be an actress.

"Well, the important thing is that you're happy," Mina says. "Right?"

After dinner, Mina goes over to Anna and Nicky's house to watch some TV. She tells me Anna won't speak English, but she loves *The Price Is Right*. "She knows how to bargain with money, that's for sure."

"Go," I say. "I'll clean the kitchen, you go."

While cleaning, I listen to Mina's tape of traditional folk songs from the Philippines. In my mind, there's a stage where a cast of servants and royalty enter. The servants carry huge bamboo poles and parasols. There is a princess held high up on a little throne. Everyone is dressed in bright colors and surrounded by black night. The princess wears a beaded dress and a veil across her face. The magic moon follows her. For a moment I see myself underneath that veil and then the phone rings and I realize I'm the one carrying the bamboo poles.

*

I sneak up to Mina's dance studio in the attic. The floors are old and creaky, but clean. There is no furniture up here save a folding stool in the corner. A boom box sits next to the chair and a few scattered cassettes lie on the floor. She has placed three full-length mirrors against one of the walls. In another corner of the room, there is a wooden chest spilling over with costumes and hats. Digging through this chest I find my grandmother's wedding dress, a traditional *Maria Clara* gown in white. There is a *terno*, a formal dress—the kind you saw Imelda Marcos in. The dress is a pale mint-green with flowers embroidered at the hem. The sleeves are high starched butterfly sleeves—the neckline is heart-shaped and sexy while still covering enough to be demure. I take the *terno* out of the chest and hold it up to my face. Mina asked for all these old dresses when my grandmother had died. I didn't want any of them. I saw no need for it. Holding the dress up with my right hand and flaring the skirt out with my left, I sway to the right, then the left. I turn in a circle.

The mirror reflects a young Filipina—brown skinned and thick lipped, short with stocky little legs. The dress is too long for her. She's a girl I've avoided. I've seen her looking for me in doorways and bus windows, but I always play dumb. She is a Chink. A Jap. A foreigner. I've felt her tapping my shoulder as I've walked down the street, but I always pretend she's not there. My friends would laugh if they saw me with her. Eddy would disown me. I know.

But standing here in front of the mirror, alone in Mina's attic, I see she's kind of pretty. I smile at her and offer her a dance.

"Are you married?" I ask the girl. She shakes her black hair. She's not. "Are you in love?" I ask the girl. She tells me she's not sure, maybe. "Are you happy?" The girl begins to cry.

*

On Saturday night, I go with Mina to her nightclub, The Babaloo, a former warehouse in the meat packing district. There is a line of ghoulish-looking people waiting at the door. Some are cloaked in leather—the women in black bustiers, the men in vests. And even more are decorated in daisies and fringe. It's the return of the ugly Seventies. Mina wears crushed-velvet fuchsia hip hugger hot pants, a midriff halter and granny boots. I'm wearing a polo shirt, walking shorts and a pair of Keds deck shoes.

"Why didn't you tell me I was dressed like a dork?" I scold her. We walk ahead of the line. "Why didn't you tell me it was a theme bar?"

"It's not a theme bar," Mina says, grabbing my arm. "Nobody cares and besides, I offered you the pick of my closet, but did you want to wear my clothes? No. Remember?" She waves to a guy in a ripped off T-shirt and leather vest. He stands officiously at the front door. "Hi Rusty," Mina says. "This is my cousin Rose."

"Hey Rosie," he grunts, "have fun."

Inside, the club is teeming with bodies—half-dressed, over-dressed, under-dressed bodies. Faces, expressionless and bored, exaggerate their features with false eyelashes, lipstick and white powder. Such costumes, I think, such masks, such attention to attitude. There's a red glow in the room, mixed with smoke from cigarettes and incense. Lava lamps decorate walls, love beads hang from ceilings and there is a dull aching beat swaying in the masses.

As we work our way through the crowd, people greet Mina, kissing her on the cheek as we go, hugging her like a long lost friend. Sometimes she introduces me, but more often than not the people pass too quickly. Worming my way through the room I try to breathe, but I feel suffocated in sweat.

"I gotta get to work," she tells me. "I'm late. Marty!" she calls, "Aggie! Come here and keep my cousin company."

A woman wearing black biker shorts and a lycra shirt approaches us with her boyfriend. He is tall, pale and sickly—or maybe it's just the light. His hair is dyed midnight.

"Hey," he says.

"I'll see you guys later!" Mina cries as she runs from us, disappearing fast into the mob.

The three of us stand there for an awkward moment, nodding our heads to the indiscernible music, a shadow of dance in our movement. I look around as if waiting for someone I know to appear.

The light in the club dims near black. Several streams of light chase across the room, like searchlights in the midst of a storm. They are above us on fire escapes and staircases. The lights settle on them. And there in the center is Mina.

She closes her eyes, hair covering the right side of her face, arms held up above her. The music enters her like a dream, like a potion, like something magic slowly coloring her every move. I can almost see the rhythm roll from her fingers through her arms and shoulders, twisting about her neck, rolling down and down. She is lost, dancing with such conviction that she hears only music.

Seeing Mina on stage makes me think of those plays I made up as a girl. Villains were my specialty. And while I enjoyed my juicy parts, my character always lost—which was okay since I was the one who had written the play, directed it and provided costumes from my mom and dad's closet. Our parents would clap when together we'd scream, "And they lived happily ever after." I was the one who always had the ideas, the one who wanted to be on stage, the actress, the star. Mina played along, but I was the actress. Later in high school, I got to play the leading roles, I was the ingenue. My mother always said that it was nice I had a hobby outside of school. A hobby, that was all it was to her. When I got a chance to act in community theater, my dad warned me not to lose sight of my priorities.

Smoke seeps out from the corners of the room, fills the air, feels like it's rising from under our feet. The bass pounds, grows so loud I think I see the walls shaking, the air around me wavering. The lights shift, and the go-go girls drape their shadows on a wall of exposed brick. Mina's shadow is gigantic, distorted. People crowd around me, singing along to the music, screaming and hooting like children on cups full of sugar. Someone slips past me, slides their palm along my bottom. Pinches. I jump. I hate Mina for bringing me here, for packing me into this room, for making me witness the way they all pay homage to her. I feel dizzy and out of breath and I'm choking from the smoke and the heat and the limp flesh of others—sticky damp, restless hands, arms, parts I don't even recognize. I feel the breath of someone on my neck, hot whiskey breath. I jam my elbow back, into a side, a torso and then I worm my way out of the crowd, out of the club.

*

Watching the blur of street lights, city lights, headlights meshed together behind my tears, I take a cab back to Mina's neighborhood. I don't understand this feeling. I only know I've got to get back to someplace safe and familiar.

When the cab lets me off, I jump out, walking quickly towards the house. As I open the gate, I hear a yawp, loud and wild. Turning quickly, I see Nicky, face full of dirt and tears streaming down the dimples of his cheeks. He is barking something at me, beating on his chest. I run from him, but he follows me, dragging his broken body. I get to the door and I realize I haven't got keys. I turn and run past Nicky, down the sidewalk, breathing hard, and weeping too.

Walking east, I move towards the lake, my arms wrapped about my body like giant bandages. On the corner there is a neighborhood bar where locals—men in greasy jean jackets and gray-stubbled beards—sit on the front stoops, waving their bottle-neck beer. I stop at a store-front window and stare at the neon red circle, at the purple lettering inside of it flashing, *Lily's Palm Reading Service*. I think about the loons who must keep Lily and her neon lights busy. On the corner of the glass pane is a card with Lily's hours. I take note. At the corner, I enter Micky's, a greasy spoon restaurant. The brash haze of fluorescent lights yellows my skin, causes me to squint. A jukebox croons country western something. Someone calls out, I think a waitress, "Hi hon." Slipping into an old-fashioned telephone booth, I pull the accordion door shut. A light pops on and I pump the phone full of silver quarters, dimes and nickels. I pump the phone full of numbers. The distant gurgle-ring of Eddy's phone burrows its way into my ear.

"Hullo?" he says.

"Hi honey, I'm so glad you're home."

"It's two in the morning."

"Eddy I want to come home. I want to get out of here. It's weird and it feels strange and I feel so out of place."

I'm sobbing, dripping tears onto the phone's mouthpiece, I can't seem to spit the words out fast enough. All I want is for Eddy to understand and bring me home. "I went to Mina's club tonight and it was smoky and people dressed like it was Halloween and she stood in front of them, practically naked, and moved around like some sex kitten and I just stood there. I got sick. She's so happy, so sure of herself. It makes me sick."

"Something you ate?"

"No Eddy, everything makes me sick. Makes me wonder what I'm doing, what we're doing."

"What?" he says teasing me. "Are you saying you want to be a go-go dancer?"

He isn't getting it. He wants to know how much I've had to drink, am I high. I'm growing louder and faster and more irritable. "Forget it," I say.

*

I walk further towards the lake. I need to see water. I need to breathe. On the way there, a gang of boys sitting on the hoods of cars makes me think of blue-jeans commercials, the kind where boys are draped over kitschy cool things, like old convertibles and fire hydrants. The kind where they stand against brick walls or wire fences. Cool and tough and sexy. This world is right out of my TV set back in Ohio, a host of unrealities, facades. I keep waiting to get back to what I know. I close my eyes now and then, but all I see are nightmares: Nicky, his twisted body screaming at me, Marty breathing black smoke into my ear, go-go dancers consumed in red light. I march past the boys, fingering my keys, ready to attack the attackers. But all they do is greet me quietly as I pass. One boy says, "*Cuidado*, it's late." I smile at them, still marching.

Down at the lake, I sit on jagged rocks and I stare out into the water until my eyes become familiar with the dark, until I start to see the definition of the waves rolling in. I try to picture Eddy. Eddy holding me. Eddy smiling. Eddy waiting for me at the gate, altar, bank. But even this distorts itself into some ugly measure of a dream. I think about my first few days here in Chicago, how I was so excited to see Mina, to find out who she is now. I wanted her to know me too, but two weeks later, and I'm not even sure of who I am.

At six o'clock I knock at Mina's door. I've been pounding for almost fifteen minutes before I hear her footsteps, and the locks as they unwind. She opens the door dressed in a T-shirt and sweatpants, her hair is ruffled and she is squinting at me.

"Hi," I whisper as I brush past her.

"Hi?" she answers me. "Hi? Where the hell have you been? Where did you go?" She's spitting out her whispers. I slip into the front hallway.

"I went for a walk."

"You went for a walk in the middle of the night. In Chicago. Do you know how worried I was? Do you know what could have happened to you?"

"Do I know?" I say. "Yeah, I do and you know what? I'm a big girl."

She hushes me and points to the living room where Nicky has fallen asleep. "He had a bad night," she tells me. Creeping slowly to the couch, I look into his face. The muscles are relaxed, soft and I think, smiling. He doesn't look like the monster I dreamt of, but a baby, innocent and quiet. Like this he is so fragile. I shudder guilt from my bones and go to the kitchen.

Mina follows me. "I was ready to call the cops."

"I needed the fresh air."

"Come on, Rosie," she says coaxing me to open up.

"Look, just 'cause I'm not beautiful and adjusted and happy like your majesty, doesn't mean there's something wrong with me. I just didn't feel like staying."

"Why are you being such a bitch?"

I reach into the cupboard and pull out a canister of coffee. I'm so angry, the can slips from my fingers and little grinds of coffee dust the kitchen counter and floor. I put the lid back on the can. "Just leave me alone, would you?"

"You want to be left alone? You come here unannounced, so I welcome you, introduce you to my friends, feed you—and you act like this is my problem, like being here is hell? Thanks, cousin."

"Well, people change, don't they?"

"What?" Mina tugs at me, rubbing gently on the blade of my shoulder.

I yank my body away from her. I raise my hand to hit her, I'm so mad. I'm screaming now. I'm telling her she's not perfect. She's too tall and too skinny and what man would want a bone like her. No wonder she's alone. I'm telling her to grow up, to get a real job, be responsible like the rest of us. "The rest of us have grown up, Mina," I tell her. "The rest of us know exactly what we're doing."

"No you don't. You don't. You've always been uptight. You've always kissed everyone's ass and now you're miserable. So don't blame me. Don't blame anyone."

Her eyes dart, wild with anger. I slump to the floor to pick up the canister and cast it at the wall. It breaks open and the grinds spill out, scatter everywhere. I fold into myself, crying. I can feel her moving towards me as she puts her arms around me, pulls me gently to her, embracing me the way my mother has, my grandmother has. The women in my family have always embraced and understood this silent way. She cries with me on the floor of the kitchen, grazing my back with the palm of her hand, rocking me gently, while Nicky, who has woken up, stumbles to the doorway, stands inside its frame and watches.

TALK TO ME, MILAGROS

On the day Milagros Bustos and her family arrived from the Philippines, my mother ran around the house with a dish towel, shooing us into action. Vacuum this, she ordered, dust that, sweep here, pick-up, pick-up, pick-up! It was Saturday, our day of rest, our cartoon morning, and Mom refused to give us any peace. Dad was at the hospital making rounds, which meant we had dibs on the television at least until lunch. My twin brothers hung upside down from the leather loveseat, punching and tickling each other at once, while my baby sister lay flat on her tummy with her favorite blanket smashed up into her face. She was still sucking her thumb then. This would not do for Mom, and when she came through the TV room waving that rag, we scattered like chicks across a barnyard.

"Your Uncle Victor and Auntie Nita will be here tonight," Mom told us. "There are nine of them in all. We need to get organized."

"What's the name of the girl my age?" I asked.

"Milagros."

Victor and Nita Bustos were not blood relatives, but they came from Dad's town, so that made them as good as family. People from Dad's province often made Peoria their first American experience, stopping in for months at a time until they could settle into homes of their own. The families were usually small in number and young. We never had this many people come over at once and I was glad to hear that there was a girl my age. I had always wanted a sister to play with. Len, my own sister, was too young to be anything but a pest. To my annoyance she followed me around, slow like a shadow turtle, repeating my words like a parrot. I liked the idea of having someone who was mature like me, who knew how to get along in the company of fifth and sixth graders.

We would talk about clothes and rock stars—I liked David Cassidy from the Partridge Family. We would talk about how to get along with our mothers and how to boss our younger siblings. I had great plans for me and Milagros.

At six that evening, my father arrived and brought with him the sounds of many feet shuffling through our kitchen door, foreign tongues speaking voice over voice, mixing orders with salutations. The Bustos clan carried leather suitcases and brown carton boxes wrapped with hemp and marked in big black letters: USA.

Auntie Nita was a short woman with a round and generous face. She kissed each of my brothers, my sister, and me, zealously, leaving heavy lipstick prints on our cheeks. She squeezed the breath out of us and rolled us in the cavity of her bosom. She smelled of fading perfume—islands and salt water drifting from her along with the musty scent of travel. She placed her seven girls before us naming them as she did.

"This is Milagros," she told us. "She is like you, Nelda," she said, pushing her slightly towards me. Milagros was small. Her skin was dark brown and her elbows stuck out at her sides like stick-figure arms. Her bald knees were dry and white. Her hair was long, a shiny blue-black midnight that covered her back like a satin curtain. I could tell that luck lived with Milagros, for above her right eye was a giant black dot. My mother had once told me that moles were a sign of good fortune. Special people with special gifts were marked by moles, and Milagros' mole was big, flashing "Lucky" like a neon sign.

"Hi," I said, but she only stared at me. Her mother told us she was shy and went on rattling off introductions. Besides Milagros there was Myette, Melina, Malu, Maritess, Maya and Monette.

"Look, Nelda," my mother said. "You and Milagros will have your hands full, babysitting all these girls as well as your own brothers and sister."

That night I brought her to my room and introduced her to my things. "Do you have your own room in the Philippines," I asked her, "or do you have to share?" Milagros sat in my rocking chair, legs drawn to her chest, head up. Her long hair shifted from her shoulders to her face as she rocked, never looking at me, never saying one word. When she didn't answer me, I went on. "You probably don't know any English, so that's okay. You'll figure it out." I walked about my room, picking up objects and explaining them to her. "These are my favorite stories," I told her, pointing to my collection of Beverly Cleary books. "Henry's a boy and Ribsy's a dog—they're friends with Ellen Tibits and Ramona the pest." I showed her my favorite pair of platform shoes, a paper flower from last summer's fair, my painted stones from the beach. Milagros sat in my chair and rocked past my show-and-tell, never looking up to see my treasures.

She walked over to her little brown suitcase and pulled something out. She stretched out her hand and offered me a photograph. The picture was black and white. It had white scalloped edges that were rough and uneven like waves in the ocean. "Who are these girls?" I asked her. The photo was taken in front of a white clay building. On the edge of the picture you could see the trunks of palm trees and huge ferns. In the middle of the picture were three rows of girls dressed in white cotton sailor dresses. They were all small like Milagros and they all had long hair tied up or brushed back in some neat fashion. "These your friends?" I asked her. She nodded.

"Here are my dolls," I said. "Crissy's my favorite 'cause you can make her hair short or long by pressing a button in back." I fingered Crissy's blond hair, which felt dry like straw. "I wish I could make my hair long or short that fast—don't you?" I pulled Milagros from the rocking chair and brought her to my vanity mirror.

In the mirror I could see that I was much taller than she, and while my skin had always been milk chocolate, I seemed pale and yellow next to Milagros. "Is that your natural skin color, or are you tan?" I asked her. I told Milagros that in the summertime all the kids on the block would lay out on the Ozowski's porch and sunbathe. I told her how my mother never let me join them, saying I was already too brown. Milagros stood perfectly still, staring at our reflection. "I think you're pretty," I said. I touched the ends of her hair which were even coarser than the doll's. "Mom keeps cutting mine." There was a gold glimmer, a sparkle, buried underneath her mane of hair, near the nape of her brown neck. I remember thinking she was a lucky girl, for she had pierced ears with two tiny pearls set in gold.

I played my Partridge Family records for her and showed her how to dance to them. I moved about my room and utilized all the floor space, weaving around the bed and rocking chair, flailing my arms like a giant bird. "Want to dance?" I asked her, but she sat back down and rocked in the chair.

During the next few weeks, she grew to like my records too. Sometimes Milagros would pull me through the house by the wrist, leading me to the bedroom. She'd point at the records underneath my turntable and I would put on the Partridge Family. Then she would sit on that chair by the window and rock. She'd rock a little faster when the needle got to songs like "I Think I Love You" and "Point Me in the Direction of Albuquerque." Sometimes I danced around the room or I stretched my body across the bed. Milagros always sat in my chair, sometimes staring out the window or down at the floor, sometimes pulling out that picture of the girls. Every now and then, I'd catch her looking at me and we'd lock eyes. I'd smile at her. She'd smile back. We always listened to the same side of the album. We listened long and hard and even though Milagros never spoke, she learned to mouth the lyrics on that record. We'd sit there until we were called to set the table or get the younger children ready for bed.

Once I asked my mother why Milagros was always so quiet. "She never talks," I complained. "She's kind of boring."

My mother told me to be patient. "It's not easy," she said as she ran her fingers through my hair. "Milagros has just left her home and all her friends. Be patient, Nelda."

My mother distributed the Bustos family into different parts of the house: Uncle Victor and Auntie Nita and the two babies slept in the extra bedroom below the kitchen. The three older Bustos girls, Milagros, Myette and Melina, stayed on the floor in my bedroom. Malu and Maritess shared the bed in Len's room.

I liked the way things were set up. At night my floors were covered with blankets, pillows, and sleeping bags. It was always a slumber party, what with bodies on the floor and giggling in the dark and secrets between Myette and Melina. Every night the ritual was the same. We bathed the children, two at a time, dried them thoroughly with mother's heavy white towels, and then dusted each one in talcum powder. My brothers and sister and the rest of the Bustos girls would meet in my bedroom where Milagros and I would lead the nightly prayers. After the prayers, just when we all should have been quieting down for sleep, came a serious round of tickling fits and pillow fights—Bustos girls against the Carreros kids.

Sometimes, after the little ones were in bed, Milagros and I sat on the stairs and watched the grown-ups. Since Uncle Victor and Auntie Nita had come over, my parents had been acting like teenagers. The four of them would sit up late at night, talking and laughing as they played many rounds of mah-jongg. They would sit at a card table, rolling the marble tiles about, building them into walls and telling jokes in *Taglish*—their own brand of *Tagalog* mixed with English.

Uncle Victor was excited to be in America. "Nita and I will build a house soon, and the girls will go to a nice Catholic school. Next year, we'll vacation in Florida."

"With what money?" Auntie Nita always wanted to know. She called her husband *ma ya bang*, which meant he was a talker, a showoff, a Mr. Big Shot. Dreamer.

My father let Uncle Victor talk, but sometimes warned him, "It's true, if you save, you can have a much better life here, Victor, but first you have to find work."

"No problem," Uncle Victor said, laughing. "This is America."

Every morning, Uncle Victor woke up at five. He showered, shaved, and slapped his face with pine-smelling aftershave. He slicked his hair back with a dab of pomade. I can still see him sitting at the edge of the sofa, dressed in his fancy grey suit, buffing the tops of his black oxford shoes as he read the morning paper. When Auntie Nita and my mother would wake up, he'd serve them coffee and eggs, with onions and fried rice. Then, waving the paper at them, he'd set off to find a job.

In the Philippines, Uncle Victor was an attorney in the city of Pitogo. His practice was strong and he had the respect of the whole community. Auntie Nita said he was famous for grand speeches in the court house and that he had won many cases solely on his wit.

"Is he looking for a job in the court house?" I asked her. But she said that he couldn't be an attorney here, not yet, since the laws back home were different from those in America. When I told Auntie Nita that I didn't understand why he left such a great job, she told me that he had done it for the girls. "They will have better opportunity here, Nelda," she assured me. "They'll have the chance to be more than wives," she told me.

Milagros looked up from her basket of laundry, tossed a cloth diaper down and shaking her head, she grumbled something in *Tagalog*. I couldn't catch all the words.

"*Ay anak*," Auntie Nita sighed. "Child, I've told you before, it's for your own good. We know what we're doing, trust, *anak*."

So Uncle Victor interviewed for jobs at department stores and restaurants. He called on small businesses.

Whenever he came home at the end of the day, he would be whistling and smiling, bearing chocolate candy bars for all the children. His baby girls would climb up his torso and my brothers would leap on to his back and chant, "Uncle Victor, Uncle Victor!" We'd cover him like ants on sugar and he would tickle us all.

"Did you find work?" I'd ask him and he would shake his head and say, "Not yet, *hija*, not yet, but soon."

Milagros was the only one who never came running. She would stand at the end of the hall and wait for the children to climb off him. Then she'd approach him, kiss him on the cheek, and hand him his slippers.

Every night when my dad got home from the hospital, he and Uncle Victor had the same conversation. They sat under the lamp in our living room, my father sinking back into the leather of his reclining chair and Uncle Victor leaning forward on the edge of the sofa. They always initiated these talks with idle banter and as the conversation took a solemn turn, the men's voices grew softer and each man perched himself closer to the end of his seat, resting his weight forward, nearly whispering into the other's ear. My dad would always get around to Uncle Victor's job hunt and Uncle Victor would lighten the conversation again. "I think that any day now, I will find something. I think that soon I will have a great job." My father always assured Uncle Victor that it was still early and that he shouldn't be discouraged if he didn't find work right away, but Uncle Victor interrupted him every time, saying, "Don't worry, this is America, I'll be working soon." Uncle Victor would not listen to negative talk, would not hear of discrimination.

Once everyone went to sleep and all you could hear was the slow methodical tumble of the washer-dryer, the whir of the dishwasher, and the occasional hum of our refrigerator, Uncle Victor would pull out his law books and spread them carefully underneath the lamp that hung over the kitchen table. While we rested, Uncle Victor murmured American laws and rules and cases to himself. Once I got up to get a glass of water and I saw him at the table, reverently whispering the Constitution out loud. Like a child memorizing prayers during Mass, he uttered every syllable. Then, checking himself for accuracy, he peered over the bridge of his glasses, into stacks of white-papered books.

*

After three weeks, things were still not clicking for me and Milagros. Sometimes I thought it was because we were too busy executing chores or watching over our siblings. It seemed we never had time to talk or get to know each other as friends were supposed to do. Every night after we rinsed the dishes and swept the kitchen floor, after we wiped the counters and before we gave the children their baths, we went to my room where I would write out my homework or read a book. Milagros had a pen pal. She wrote a letter every night. Then every day she'd check the mailbox for letters and slip the one she wrote into the silver box.

"Who are you writing to?" I asked her once. "One of your friends?" She covered up the note with her free hand and pressed her face close to the desk, scribbling her perfect tiny letters fast. Maybe she thought if she wrote small enough and fast enough, I wouldn't be able to see who she was writing to. She kept a stack of letters written on light blue paper in her purse. The handwriting was angular and jagged so that the L's looked like right triangles and the capital G's were rectangles with wings. I was jealous of the way she poured words onto the letters she wrote, of how she hoarded the ones from the Philippines as though she were all alone in America.

Her eyes, two big black dots glaring, seemed masked and disguised from me and my understanding. I often found her looking at me and it seemed she didn't care. She never looked away. She never seemed embarrassed or awkward like me.

Sometimes when Milagros and I babysat, she spoke to her sisters in *Tagalog*. She must have been telling them stories, for they would settle around her, hanging onto her sleeve or her leg. They'd braid the long black strands of her hair, responding to her words in sighs and gasps and brittle bits of laughter. Even Len, who couldn't understand a word Milagros said, fell victim to the rhythm of her voice, a voice that rose and fell like water running along the rocks of a river.

The funny thing was, I often heard Auntie Nita speak to

Milagros in English—"Change Monette's diaper" or "Make some rice" or "Tell your *tita* I'm here." Milagros always obeyed her, never speaking back, never asking her mother to repeat the words. Once when we were sitting on the steps, watching the children play a game of tag, I asked her why she wouldn't speak back in English.

She turned to look at me through strands of hair that fell into her brown face. She looked like an island girl to me, someone pretty and exotic. She pushed her hair away from her face and revealed her beautiful pearl earring. Shrugging, she said, "*Ay wong ko.*" She didn't know. Then one of the little ones fell and she was off, reprimanding them for playing so rough. "*Tama na!*" she told them, pulling one sister off of another. "Enough!"

*

One Sunday, we had a barbecue in our backyard. My father invited people from his hometown who might know the Bustos family, as well as those he thought should know them. Many of these people had stayed with us at one time or another when they first got to the States. These events were practically a circus with many voices speaking at once, and bodies small and large moving about in circles.

We roasted a pig on a spit in the backyard. The men took turns spinning the pig while the women kept bringing food out to a long table in the shade. We had two card tables set up for poker or mah-jongg. The Reyes brothers brought an acoustic guitar and a set of bongo drums and sang Philippine love songs to our families. My parents had a way of encouraging talk from everyone, talk that happened at once, talk that often went unheard. For us, noise was a sign of happiness and *fiesta*.

Milagros and I wandered about the party, weaving in and out of people in silence. We went from table to table, watching the women rapidly flipping mah-jongg tiles to the center of the table, taking long drags from their unfiltered cigarettes, and blowing smoke from the corners of their painted mouths.

For a while we sat in front of the Reyes brothers and listened to them—their voices were soft, sliding from one note to the next like lounge singers crooning in an Elvis bar. Tony Reyes stood in front of us wearing a pair of bell-bottom denims and a flowered shirt that he left unbuttoned. His crucifix swung as he strummed and sometimes you could hear Jesus banging across the instrument's wood, echoing into the hollow of the guitar.

Sitting cross-legged in front of the Reyes brothers, I leaned into Milagros' ear and whispered, "Are they cute?"

She giggled back and said, *"Hindi naman!"* which meant, no way.

We watched the older men roasting the *baboy* on the spit. In the center of the circle, Uncle Joe, an old timer who first came to the u.s. in 1920, sat on an old tree stump. His legs were thrown apart and he leaned his elbows on the top of his thighs, shaking his pipe and nudging the brim of his straw cap.

"When I first came to this country," he told them, "I lived in San Francisco. There were restaurants that had signs on the doors: Absolutely No Filipinos. Back then they called us *Pinoys*, monkeys, you know. Work was hard to come by. *Ay naku*, it was really something."

"I don't believe it," Uncle Victor said.

"You see, I thought that too because that is what they tell us back home—America land of opportunity." He shook his head, clicking his tongue, and confessed, "I was so homesick, I almost gave up twice—once in 1937 and then again in forty-two. I just wanted to get back home."

When we had enough of the hoopla, Milagros and I wandered back into the house, me, to sit at the edge of my bed paging through my latest copy of *Teen Beat*, and Milagros to rock my chair.

I looked at her and thought of times in the middle of the night when I had heard her sniffling to herself. "Milagros," I'd call. "Are you okay?"

"Hindi na bali," she'd say. Never mind.

"Why?" I'd ask her. *Bakit?* She never had an answer.

I ran my hands along the pages of my magazine, pretending that the photo of David Cassidy was real. I held the picture up to her.

"Do you think he's handsome?" I asked her. "Do you think that he might like me, I mean if he met me?" She looked at me with that heart-shaped faced, framed by her neatly parted hair, and smiled. "You don't think so?" I asked. I went to the mirror and examined myself. My pixie-cut hair stood up on its ends—down by my neck trailed little wisps of hair frayed and loose like David's own shag hairdo. My big teeth stuck out from under my lip, dressed in silver bands—braces that promised to mold my mouth into something pretty and petite. On the bridge of my nose, a pair of psychedelic plastic glasses helped me see far away. My body was stick straight, thin like a boy's, so thin that when I turned sideways, people said they couldn't see me. I was cloaked in cotton—a pair of pants with colorful prints like bright yellow pineapples and purple bananas, blue apples and orange watermelons. My shirt was a ribbed sleeveless turtleneck with blue piping around the armpit. Mom had bought it from the summer rack in the Ladies' department at Gimbel's. I was wearing a bra that my mother had bought—it was padded and much too big for my eleven year old body, but I wore it anyway. I turned to Milagros and told her I thought maybe David Cassidy would think she was the pretty one.

When she didn't answer me, I began to get annoyed. I walked over to the rocking chair and asked her, "Why won't you speak? Why won't you ever answer me?" I pushed the back of the chair, rocking her faster as I spoke. "Say something. Tell me to shut up. You're in America now, you know: we speak English here. What's the matter with you?"

Milagros drew her lips into a straight line and wrapped her fingers around the handles of the rocking chair. "Your mother speaks to you in English—she told me they teach English at your little convent school in the Philippines—why won't you talk it?" I shoved the chair harder, trying my best to make her answer me. I pushed again and again. But she stayed there, sitting, sturdy as ever.

Then I went to the closet where she hung her purse and I

pulled out the stack of air-mail letters. She jumped up then, scratching at me, prying the letters from my hands. I threw them up and they sailed across the room like a flurry of giant snowflakes.

Milagros bit her lip, grabbed my hands, and leaned her weight against mine. We stood for a moment, pressing up against our invisible walls, tummy to tummy, palm against palm. I was tired of being the nice hostess. I was sick of having this girl in my house. Even though this was my house, she was the one who got all the attention now—"See how Milagros can cook? See how Milagros can bathe all her sisters? Isn't Milagros beautiful?" Milagros and her lucky mole or not, this was my house, not hers, the least she could do was talk to me. I locked my hands with hers and dug my nails into her cocoa-brown skin. Her hair tumbled into her face, strayed into the corners of her mouth, and stuck.

Milagros growled at me, tightened the muscles in her face. "*Bastus Americana!*" she said.

"What do you know about Americans," I asked. "You're the stupid one. You can't even talk English. You know what? I don't want to be your friend. Go back to your little group of girlfriends!"

Tears pooled in her black eyes, rolled down her face, and streaked across the slope of her cheek. "You cry baby," I said, "go back to the Philippines. Go back to where you belong!"

Just as Milagros began to fall, Len came toddling into the room. "Your mommy wants you," Len told Milagros. "She wants you to dance."

*

Down in the backyard, Auntie Nita lined up five of her seven girls (Maya and Monette were still babies). They stood in a straight line, waiting for the music, and as the drone of the ukelele began, the Bustos girls twirled their hips and rotated their wrists. They shuffled their feet right then left and swayed to the strains of Don Ho's song, "Tiny Bubbles."

Milagros led her sisters in the dance, swaying up ahead of them to encourage them, remind them, show them how to do it.

She curled her fingertips, then stretched them out, allowing a wash of ukelele mixed with Don Ho's croon to move through her hand, then forearm and elbow and shoulder. The sisters moved together and stirred the air like gentle waves rippling onto sandy beaches. Milagros moved her hips in a circle.

"That's called around the island!" Auntie Nita told everyone.

Then Milagros' movements grew big and her arms stretched through space, rearranged the atmosphere, popped the tiny bubbles. The other sisters followed Milagros as they seemed to float among our guests and turn our Midwest garden into a tropical paradise.

I watched the eyes of our friends and neighbors. Everyone at the party had stopped to watch the Bustos girls. Conversations were traded for sighs and exclamations. "*Ganda!*" they gasped. And they were right, the five little island girls were beautiful. They told a story about Don Ho's tiny bubbles that made him feel happy, made him feel fine. Who cares? I thought. What a dumb song.

A few of the women tried coaxing me to join the sisters, but I had never taken a dance lesson in my life, much less hula lessons. There was no way I was going to dance up there next to Milagros and there was no way that I could ever forgive her for standing up in the middle of my backyard and dancing.

*

That night, after everyone had gone, Milagros and her mother sat in the corner of the living room, talking quietly. Milagros fingered the photo of her friends and occasionally held it out to her mother. I watched their bodies cast giant silhouettes against our white walls, their shadows melting in and out of each other. Milagros cried, placed her head onto her mother's lap, while Auntie Nita clicked her tongue and sighed. "*Ay naku,*" she whispered. "You'll see, *hija*, things will get better. Don't worry, *naman*." She kissed the top of Milagros' head and told her, "Enough now, daughter, *Tama na*." And Milagros nodded, Okay.

*

Whenever we were given a chore to do together, she would lead the work and I would follow. She knew how to do more than I did. Her mother let her fold the laundry and iron. She was allowed to use the stove. These were things my mother had always taken care of and so I let Milagros take the lead, since she seemed to know what she was doing.

I know these were only chores to Milagros, but for me it was like playing house. I was always amazed when the rice that we put in the pan and covered with water turned out fluffy and light. I loved that an article of clothing covered with mud from the garden could be whitened with bleach and come out new. Sometimes we stitched old pieces of fabric together and stuffed them with holey socks and nylons to make throw pillows. Before Milagros, I took all this for granted.

Sitting at the kitchen counter while my mother washed chicken parts, I asked her how come Milagros knew so much.

"It's different in the Philippines," she said. "Because life's harder back there, girls learn early how to do housework, how to help."

"I thought everyone had maids," I said.

"A lot of people do," my mother said. "But still, the Philippines is old-fashioned that way, you know. Girls learn how to do women's work and boys learn to do men's work."

"Why don't you want me to help?" I asked her as I doodled on the corner of my homework.

"Maybe I've spoiled you, ha, *hija?*"

"Maybe," I said. I thought about the way Milagros was always so serious, how she never seemed to want to play. Maybe, I thought, it's because they never gave her time to play in the Philippines. She was too busy working.

*

Tuesday Uncle Victor came home, while Mom and Auntie Nita were at the grocery store. He came into the house whistling as he always did, giving us chocolate too. We went through the rituals we had established with him, the children crawling all over him, the slipper thing with Milagros, everything. It had been two months since they had arrived.

"Where did you go today?" I asked.

"I went to the shopping mall," he told us. "I talked to the man at the shoe store, the lady at the dress shop, the book store. I spoke to somebody at a place where they sold little silver and gold trinkets with engravings."

"Did you go to the jewelry store?" I wanted to know.

Uncle Victor nodded his head. "I did."

"Did they need a lawyer?" my brother asked.

"Well, children," Uncle Victor announced. "It looks like someone needed a lawyer!"

Myette, Melina and Maritess danced around their father, pulling on his pants leg and kissing his hands.

"Really, Uncle Victor?" asked one of my brothers.

"Yes, *hijo*, really! Elroy's Easy Diner."

I looked at Milagros and smiled at her. "This is good, huh? Aren't you glad?" She smiled stiffly at me.

"Okay, *na*," she said.

Uncle Victor swooped down to cradle Milagros in his thick arms. "*Hija*," he said. "Aren't you gonna kiss me congratulations?" Milagros nodded her head, leaned into his cheek and kissed.

"Congratulations, Papa," she told him.

"Soon," Uncle Victor told her, "I will pass the law review and I can start my own practice. You and the girls will go to a nice school and have lots of pretty clothes. You'll see, *hija*, you'll see." He put his face against hers, and spun her around the room.

"Okay, Papa," she said. "Okay."

*

A week later, Milagros and I decided to visit her father at Elroy's Easy Diner. We walked along the boulevard in silence. The sun was out, warming my face, and a spring breeze blew secrets past my ear. I was not in the mood to talk, so I kept my eyes fixed on the path in front of me. I dragged my toe, marking the dirt behind me, scuffing my new red tennis shoe. I hummed under my breath, rattled lyrics to myself.

"Aren't you excited?" I asked her. "Aren't you excited to see your dad at work? They don't let kids in hospitals, so I've never seen my dad at work. Plus, your dad'll give us treats."

"It's okay," she said.

"Hey, Nelda!" called a voice. "Hey, you stuffer!"

There in the hollow of the creek stood Trent Collins, a neighborhood boy, and with him were Carrie Shamanski, Mark Checkolinski, Amy Owlrick, and Stanley Martin, the boy I had a crush on. Trent ran up to me and snapped my bra. "So you still stuffing?"

"I do not stuff!" I yelled. It wasn't my fault that this bra my mother bought didn't fit me, it had been on sale.

"What?" Stanley asked.

"Yeah," Trent said as he danced around me, "Nelda the Nerd, stuffs—look, can't you see?" He lurched forward, thrust the palm of his hand onto my chest.

The sun was glaring into the lens of my glasses, and so I had to squint. The children stood frozen like shadows in a game of statues, staring at me. I swung my arm, which was as thin as a sapling, at Trent. I heard them laugh at my attempt. Someone said something about my clothes. Someone said something about my nerdy little Chinky glasses that went with my nerdy little Chinky face—I don't know who because the sun had blurred their horrid little mouths—maybe they all said it. Maybe they said it at once, together, several times. I looked down at my chest and I could see the crinkled little cup-cakes of my padded bra smashed across my chest, my cotton pants ballooning out into the afternoon wind. I swung again. I missed.

Milagros leapt from behind me, tossed a stone at the group of children, broke the spell.

"Leave Nelda alone," she said as she rubbed her hands. "You are *bastus* for teasing my friend." She held up her fist, ready to fight, but I grabbed her sleeve, pulling her close to me.

"What?" Trent said laughing. The rest of the gang scattered, leaving him alone in the ditch.

One of the kids called to him, warning him, "Let's go, Collins. Let 'em alone all ready."

Milagros turned to me and smiled, "You know *bastus?*" she asked, steering me in the direction of the diner.

"Stupid?"

"Yes, he is stupid," she said.

We fell back into silent step, me with Milagros, or Milagros with me. I looked at her and for the first time, I felt I understood.

"You went to an all-girl school in the Philippines?" I asked her. She nodded.

"You were kind of lucky," I told her. "At least girls don't snap each other's bras."

"Oh, yes," Milagros said, smiling. "Sometimes."

*

At the diner, Uncle Victor welcomed us, calling out our names as he wiped his hands off onto his apron. Uncle Victor was busy, but he brought us both a brownie and milk. I told Uncle Victor what had happened at the creek.

"Don't worry," he said. "Don't pay attention to those kids. They just don't understand."

"Do you know what they call me?" I asked him. "Nerdy Nelda."

"What is nerdy?" he wanted to know.

Milagros explained it to him in *Tagalog:* To be a nerd is to be a geek, a hang-around-with-the-book-crowd kind of individual.

"Oh," he said as he rubbed my shoulder with the palm of his hand. "You know, Nelda, nerds do very important things—they invent gadgets and machinery, they discover great cures and write beautiful poems."

Looking into his face, the roundness of his cheeks and the soft and easy comfort of his dark eyes, I thought Milagros resembled her father. She had his eyes, his manner. "I know," I told him. "That's what my mother always says."

"Hey," someone called from the other side of the diner. "Could I get some coffee here, or what?" Uncle Victor looked around but the waiter was in back—he must have been in the bathroom. Two men sat on the other side of the diner. One was huge—two hundred-some pounds. He wore a checkered shirt underneath a black windbreaker with the word "Goodyear" painted in yellow-gold letters. His jeans were baggy and worn to almost white with splotches of dirt woven into its threads. The other man was smaller, older and full of wrinkles. He had on a pair of black plastic glasses.

Uncle Victor waved at the man and smiled. He got up to get the waiter at the back of the restaurant. "One minute, sir," Uncle Victor said.

Milagros grabbed onto my wrist, squeezed. She was holding her breath. I turned to the man, as if ready to say something, but Milagros pinched me and shook her head no.

The waiter came out from back, carrying a pot of coffee. "I got it, Victor," he said. "I'll take care of it."

Uncle Victor smiled weakly at the waiter and after that he went back to bussing tables.

*

Later that night, Milagros and I stood on stools in my mother's kitchen, peeling potatoes. After a while I heard a heavy thumping sound that was constant and loud. It seemed to shake the walls and echo within the framework of our house.

"Where's your father?" Auntie Nita asked Milagros. "Is that him?" Without looking up from her work, Milagros nodded her head. "*Ay naku*," whispered Auntie Nita. "Not again." Then she calmly went to Uncle Victor. "Watch the kids, ha, Milagros?"

Soon I could also hear an occasional moan, like a wolf that had been trapped. I looked at Milagros who was intent on peeling her potatoes.

"Don't you hear that?" I whispered. "What is that?"

She picked up another potato and rinsed it. Taking the peeler in her right hand she began to shave its skin off.

I shook her shoulder. "What's the matter with you?" I yelled. I put my work down and ran to the extra bedroom.

The drumming against the wall felt heavy and full of pain. I could hear my uncle crying, sobbing, sometimes quietly and at other times howling. Auntie Nita's voice sang in a dialect I could not comprehend. Her lullaby was low and soothing. Soon she hushed his muttering.

I stood at the door, wanting to peek, wanting to know what was the matter, but I couldn't move. I'd never heard a man cry like that. I thought everything was going well now. Hadn't he found what he had been looking for? A job? In America?

My mother hissed at me to get away from the door. "Leave them alone," she warned. "That is none of your business."

But the door cracked open just then and light shed onto the walls outside of their room. I stepped up to the door and peeked in.

Auntie Nita was rubbing Uncle Victor's shoulder, pulling him gently towards her, but he wouldn't let her hold him. Instead he was cracking his head against the wall, again and again and again. His face was red, swollen and washed with tears. Uncle Victor wailed and I heard a sound rising from some deep, dark place.

Milagros pushed passed me, opened the door. She helped her mother pull Uncle Victor from the wall, helped Auntie Nita place his head on her mother's lap, ran her small hand up and down the curve of his spine, kissed him, and pressed her cheek to his shoulder. Then Milagros stood and pulled me out the door. She wiped her eyes with the back of her hand, dragging tears across her face. "He will be okay," she said.

I studied the black at the center of her eye, how the color seemed to swirl deep into forever. I wanted to stay, so when she leaned her slight body against the heavy wooden door I reached out and tried to hold it open. I pushed. The door rocked between us, was suspended in mid-air for a few seconds, but she was stronger than I. "Don't worry, Nelda," she said. "Never mind."

Then she closed the door and I stood there and stared at the knots, at the faces that ran from the wood's swirling grain, at the eyes and teeth and giant sized moles, and I waited.

BABY LUST

The house wakes to the sound of her tears running quietly down the windowpane, to her voice pushing gently on the glass, to her body rocking the trees, the pressure of her hands raking against the branches of the willow tree they had planted in the yard. The dreams have kept her awake and crying all night long.

Sitting at the kitchen table, she pours her energy into a single cup of tea. Her tears spill from the cup, into the kettle, seemingly spill into the sink and out of a tub full of water. They haven't slept for days. They haven't spoken, not really, only fought.

When the kettle howls, she knows it's time, uncomfortable as that might be, she knows she must see him. Mark shuffles his bare feet across the wooden hallway and onto the cold linoleum. The rain has seeped into the house through a crack in the window, runs sideways along the kitchen floor. She has placed a towel at the window's ledge, but the rain still seeps through.

He runs his finger along the windowpane, catches moisture there and puts it to his lips and tastes. "Did you sleep much?" he asks.

Isabel reaches for his coffee mug. "Tea?" she answers.

"I didn't," he says. "All that rain beating down like that, who could sleep?"

"Yep," she says pouring water into a porcelain tea pot. "Who could sleep." Last night, the rain leaked into her dreams, drizzled a pool of water into her sleeping uterus. She saw a tiny baby swimming in the cavern of her body, trying very hard to surface, to lift its head, to breathe. But it was too small, too weak, too young and her water refused to break. The baby drowned. She's had that nightmare each night since the miscarriage. Yes, who could sleep?

He slips his arms about her waist, pulls the ties taut on her terry-cloth robe. He peeks around her to catch a glimpse of her eye, to brush her lips with a kiss, but she refuses to look at him. As Mark buries his face into the nest of her hair, he says, "Maybe you should talk to Frankie about this. Maybe you could work it out better with your brother than me."

She shakes her head, no. She doesn't think she can tell her brother this without breaking his heart too. And why would she want to do that? It isn't the kind of thing she cares to discuss. With anyone.

This was not the right time. With another year of school, they'd rather wait. But when it happened, she was secretly happy. Mark confessed he was too. They planned to keep the baby. To work it out. Maybe they'd marry, maybe not, but they liked the idea of a child. And just as they had begun to see this third person in their life, get used to the idea of sharing their space and time with him or her, the baby floated away.

They stand there a moment, looking out the window. The rain blurs the trees. It's raining everywhere. She doesn't answer him. She doesn't move. Neither knows what to do.

*

The next day she's at that same window, staring out past the dust and mud-stained screen. She listens to the cars, the whir of the tires slipping past the house, listens to the voices of children at the corner. There is a park down the block, and from the window she can see the swings and the jungle gym, she can see children running from the slide to the sandbox. She can even hear them giggling and shouting at each other. "Duane who?" she hears. "Duane the bathtub, I'm dwowning." At least she thinks she can from here. And so she watches out that window. The sun has dried up everything, Isabel thinks, you can't even tell that yesterday there was rain. She wonders if the sand is still damp—if children would consider that good for packing into buckets and shoveling into strainers.

Across the street a young man pushes a blue stroller with a little sun roof. The man is tall and slender, dressed in long shorts and a university sweatshirt. He could be Mark, she thinks. He's built just like him. She squints, but cannot see the baby inside. She moves a little to the right of the window to get a better angle, but all she sees are the baby legs, kicking up at the air. He stops when a bootie flies off the tiny foot. He reaches down for the shoe, leans over the stroller so she can't see the child at all. He does this, seemingly in front of the house, just parallel to her window. He starts to walk again, pushing the stroller down the block, moving closer to the park. And when she sees the bootie fall from the carriage and when this time he continues walking, she pounds at the window, calls out to him.

*

Isabel spends a week in bed. It isn't that she can't get up; she won't. She covers herself up with flannel pajamas and electric blankets. "I'm so cold," she tells Mark, even though it's springtime and unusually warm.

"You've got to get better," he says as he lifts a spoon of wonton soup to her lips. "You need to get over this. You have finals and papers. There isn't time to mope."

Mope, she thinks? Is that what he calls this? "Don't you realize we've had a death?" she says to him. "Don't you feel this too?"

Sure he does, he tells her, he just doesn't see the point in moping, though he's trying very hard to understand. She wants to pick a fight with him, shake some of this depression onto him, but she already sees how he feels. He broods. He walks around the house, watering plants, over and over until they practically drown and die. He polishes the windows almost every day, has bought rags and extra bottles of window cleaner. He's obsessed, she thinks.

*

Isabel interns at a nearby elementary school as a visiting artist, teaching children history and literature and science through drama. On Presidents' day, she brought a box of wigs and frilly white shirts, knickers and hats—three-cornered ones, top hats, and others. She placed the box in the middle of the room and the children dressed her up to be George Washington and Lincoln. She even had a rubber mask of Nixon in the box.

Today she walks into the gym, after two weeks of hiding. She couldn't stand to come before today. The second graders come running at her, a herd of pint-sized running backs ready to tackle her. "Isabella!" they call. "Isabella, where were you? We missed you!" They swarm about her, buzzing at once, telling her everything. What they did, how they did it, who wronged who. Two weeks of catching up, they have so much to tell her. She plugs her ears and says, "It's so loud in here, I can't hear any of you. It's so loud my ears are going to pop."

She sits on the floor and they drop down on their knees, every single one of them, plop, plop, plop. Sunlight from the windows streams over the tops of their heads, warms the room. "If you guys wouldn't talk so much," she tells them, "I'd swear you were angels, but who ever heard of winged blabber-mouths?"

They stop speaking almost at once, their voices dying in little echoes throughout the gym. "We're angels, Isabella, hear?" says Antonya. She is a small girl with a rash of red cherub curls and a face tinted with freckles. Of course she's an angel, Isabel thinks, what else could she be?

"Watch," says Isabel as she rises up slowly. She moves in exaggerated steps. Her arms swing from side to side in slow motion, spin in circles like human propellers. She turns her head gently left then right. "I'm walking on the moon," she whispers. "I'm walking on the moon and there, that shadow comes from Earth. Who'll walk with me?" The hands go up silently and shake at her, "I will, I will." She pulls the children up slowly, guiding them gently onto the surface of the moon. "Watch out for crevices," she tells them. "Try not to fall in. Watch that you don't float right out into the universe," she warns them, afraid they might. "Stay close." They slip, slide, and glide their way across the golden moon, "Stay close," she tells them.

*

Isabel dreams her mother is sitting on her throne, a white rocking chair with little pink hearts painted on the armrests. She is five and kneeling at her mother's side, touching and groping her belly, speaking to it, blessing it, amazed that she was ever housed in such cramped quarters.

"So the baby's inside," she asks. "Right here?" Her mother nods. "And I was? And Frankie? And if I want someday I could have a baby like this? Inside me?"

"Sure," her mother says. "I would love to be a *lola*."

"Let me see," Isabel tells her.

Her mother lifts her cotton blouse up and exposes her belly. It's round like a beach ball, brown like clay, like earth. Isabel runs her dark hand along the equator of her mother's tummy. It feels firm and strong, unripe like a green avocado. Placing her cheek on her mother's stomach, she listens for the heartbeat. She hears gurgling like water spitting from a drain pipe. She hears the squish-squash of breakfast—pancakes and fresh strawberries, two glasses of whole milk—sliding towards the baby. She hears bongos hiccupping inside the chamber of her mother's stomach. Isabel rubs it as if it were a gypsy's crystal ball.

"I see her," Isabel whispers. "Two hands, two arms, two feet. Long beautiful black hair. Dimples. A girl."

Then, as suddenly as on TV, as crazy as a cartoon, there's a whoosh, and out from the side of her mother, the baby pokes its hand, or its foot, or something, destroying the perfectly round sphere of her belly, conducting an earthquake of sorts. A foot scrapes under the sheet of Mom's stomach and ripples the skin. "She's moving!" Isabel screams. "She's wild!"

She places her lips squarely onto where she imagines the baby's face, she kisses. The baby slips out of her mother like a child on a water slide. Isabel puts out her arms, trying to catch her, but the baby's too wet, too slippery, and she misses.

*

She goes on walks to the park nearly every day, sitting on benches and watching the children. They're so cute, she thinks. Sometimes she spies on young mothers and how they speak to their babies, how they discipline them and play with them and change their diapers right there in front of everyone.

Max, Frankie's baby, a boy as big as a sack of potatoes with a face round as grapefruit, fills Isabel's parents' house with toys and diaper bags, wipes, lotions, and bottles. He doesn't even live there, and the boy runs the place. He looks like that one, she thinks. A young mother places her boy in the sandbox where he crawls and scratches the dirt, makes it fly all over the little girl sitting next to him. The girl, who is maybe a year old, sits straight up, startled by the sand in her eye. She rubs at it and cries.

"He's as big as my kitty," Isabel says.

The mother looks up at her and says, "What?"

"Your baby. He's as big as my kitty, but he has a face like my nephew. Very cute." She has taken to carrying her cat, Hank, in the crook of her arm. Sometimes when Mark isn't home she'll even hum lullabies to him. The cat has figured her out and runs from Isabel every chance he gets.

*

The dreams keep her up all night and all day. Sometimes she finds herself down the block, sitting on the cold metal steps of the merry-go-round, or swinging in one of the tires. Tonight she sits on the edge of the slide, just close enough to falling, but still perched safely on its edge. The moon, golden and full, draws her eye. It is a pregnant moon, she thinks. Swollen like the sea when tide is high. It is a fertile moon.

Last weekend she and Mark went to the community spring *fiesta*. Right in the middle of the festivities—between a performance of the *tinikling* and the light dance—just as the bamboo poles caught the dancer's ankle and made her trip unexpectedly, one of the old aunts, *Tita* Betty, grabbed Isabel's hands and said, "So when are you two going to marry and have babies? You better hurry," she told Mark. "She is no spring chicken."

Mark took *Tita* Betty's comment in stride. She was known to say things like that to all the young people. She had said the same thing last Christmas at the auxiliary dance. But Isabel had ripped her wrists from *Tita* Betty's grip. Had turned away from her abruptly and yelled, "The light dance is up, I've always loved the light dance."

There was a slender young woman on stage, balancing a lighted candle on her head. Two candles in glasses flickered in her palms as she swayed and she rolled to the pulse of the music. She brought the candles up over her head, and twisted her arms, always in control of the light. Two little children danced on either side of her. A boy, in cropped pants and a white shirt, a little red bandanna tied at his neck and the girl in a plaid cotton dress with stiff butterfly sleeves at her shoulders and a red sash about her torso, carried their candles in kerchiefs and swung them gently to the music. The girl, like the woman dancing, had drawn her hair up in a bun.

Isabel knew how to dance this dance of lights. She learned to balance the candles carefully so that the wax would not dribble from the center of the flame. She had always been so good at it. And seeing the dancers, she cried. Isabel caught the tears, snuffed them out quickly, with the backs of her hands.

She told *Tita* Betty that she was touched. "The older I get," she said, "the more important these things are."

"This isn't exactly safe," says Mark. Isabel looks away from the moon and standing at the bottom of the slide, she sees him. He is barefoot and his hair stands up at the ends like one of those muppets on *Sesame Street*—Guy Smiley or Bert. He's still in his boxer shorts and T-shirt.

"You want to get hauled in for indecent exposure?" she asks. She thinks he looks like a seven-year-old boy, up from an afternoon nap.

"You should wake me, if you want to go walking at night."

"You were sleeping," she says.

Sliding her legs down the cold, slippery ramp, she kisses him. He kneels at the mouth of the slide and cradles her feet in his hands.

"It's actually better this way," he says. "We weren't planning on having a baby for a long time anyhow."

"I know." She pulls his hair at the top of his head. "But I like the idea of one. One little baby. One to keep. I didn't think I wanted a baby till we lost her."

"You think it was a her?"

Isabel shrugs her shoulders. "Not really sure. Maybe." Then she slides her legs around his waist and wraps her arms about his head, cuddling his face in the heart of her. "Could've gone either way, I guess," she tells him.

*

At the grocery store Isabel picks up several cup-of-soup meals, tomatoes, oranges, and some noodles for pasta—her favorite easy dish. She strolls by the magazine rack and tosses a couple of baby magazines into the cart. Two months ago, she had begun to research the latest parenting trends. One thing she had learned was that you shouldn't make children dependent on your approval. Ultimately, this damages their self-esteem. When a baby puts his toys away don't say, "Good boy," say, "How does putting your toys away make you feel?"

Flipping through a new issue of *Parenthood*, she pushes the cart down the aisle and nearly collides with an old man. His cart is full of canned foods, corn and peas and apricot slices. She practically knocks him down. Tossing the magazine among her own supplies, she mumbles an apology and helps him gain his balance.

A pregnant woman pushes past Isabel and the old man. Isabel notes that in her cart are bundles of diapers, milk bottles, megaboxes of Cheerios cereal, and a toddler.

The baby is a skinny girl wearing a slight pony-tail with more hair out of the rubber band than in. Her legs dangle from the cart in a continuous rhythm. Every so often she knocks her mother's swollen belly with the toe of her red tennis shoe.

"Honey, you're hurting Mama," says the woman. "I asked you to stop that." The toddler kicks again, wham, right in the center of her stomach. "Emma, I said stop." The baby claps her hands together and laughs. "Yeah," she tells her, "such a funny girl."

The young woman's voice trails off as she pushes the cart away from Isabel, who, after dusting the man off, wheels the cart around and follows the mother and child.

A voice from tin can speakers announces specials of the week, a clean-up in aisle seven, a lost child at checkout five. The voice is muffled and discernibly bored. Isabel follows a few paces behind the pregnant woman. She studies her legs, which are fitted in black leggings, how they flow from the thighs to the calves and swell into little pillars at her ankles. She strains to hear them. "Emma," says the woman. "Don't open that here. Put that down, okay. Mama will give you cookies later, after she buys it, now put that down." The child sticks her arms out on either side of the cart and grabs a sponge from the shelf, knocking over several boxes of steel wool pads. The mother stops the cart, and flustered she puts the boxes back, saying all the while, "Emma, keep your hands in the cart, honey." Emma laughs at her mom and reaches over to knock a few more packages from the shelf. Handiwipes. She giggles and her mother shouts, "Emma!"

Isabel runs to pick up the scattered boxes. "She's adorable," she tells the mother. Berry juice stains the baby's mouth, wide and free like clown makeup. Snot coats her nostrils, trickles down her lip, and into her mouth. "She really is just adorable."

"Not today," the woman says. The mother grapples with sponges and soap pads in one hand, with the other she steers the cart. Emma reaches out and rubs the swelling of her mother's abdomen which is ripe and luscious as a bowl of red grapes.

Oh I want one, Isabel thinks, I really want one. "How old is she?" Isabel asks, handing her a box. She reaches down to the floor. "Here, I got it."

"Old enough to mess with me," says the woman. "She's two."

"Well she's beautiful," Isabel tells her. "Really she is."

She shops twelve or so paces behind the woman and her baby, all the while thinking how lucky the woman is, all the while making believe she is the one pregnant with baby in cart. At the checkout line, she stands right in back of them and makes eyes at Emma. "Oh she's a little flirt," Isabel tells the mother, "isn't she?"

*

The first time it was an accident, but now Isabel seduces Mark every chance she gets. "Wouldn't it be fun," she tells him. "A little guy or a sweetie pie?" She fills their sunken tub with hot bubbles. Perfumes the water with dried rose petals. He often comes home to see her lounging in a bath, drinking a glass of fumé blanc. White candles flicker about the bathroom tiles, casting long exaggerated shadows of her arms and legs. Sometimes it works, but most times, they end up fighting.

"It's a stupid idea," he tells her. "We're not ready."

"But don't you remember how excited we were when we thought —"

"Why are you insisting on this, Bella? Why now?"

Why not is what she wants to say, but of course she knows he wants more than that. Well, honestly, she doesn't really want to think about it, she just wants to do it. Make one, and watch it grow.

*

Isabel calls Frankie, but he is never there and he never returns her calls. He's mister big shot head auto mechanic—works all day, then stays up late with the baby. Rachel says he never sleeps, let alone answers his phone calls.

One Sunday, when the family is together at Mom and Dad's, Frankie sits in front of her, reading.

"What's up?" he says, as he pages through the sports.

She wants to shake him, break this wall of Sunday papers, say, "My baby died." She wants to tell him that she has not dealt with this miscarriage, that it has almost split her and Mark up twice now, but Frankie seems too absorbed in the scoreboards. "So, did the Bucks win again or what?" she asks.

"Naw, they got trounced."

She wonders what he would say if she told him.

"How's Mark?" he asks.

"Not so great." She almost says more. She almost says, "*Because we spent a miserable week weeping and I don't think we could ever do that again.*"

"What, you mean you broke up?"

"No."

"That's good, he's kind of a meatball, but I still think he's good for you." He takes a swig of his cappuccino and says, "This coffee's too strong."

"How are you?" Isabel asks. "How's the baby?"

*

She dreams of cups of soup—the kind you just add water to. In the styrofoam she sees little bits of vegetables floating to the top—loose kernels of corn, carrots and peas. This cup has tiny shrimp. Baby shrimp. Embryos. The woman from the grocery store stands next to her, says, "It's for women who have a hard time carrying babies to term. Just add water."

Isabel holds the cup close to her face, watches the little shrimp grow tiny hands, a sleeping face, a smile. She spoons the baby out, places him in a shoe box full of things—old pictures and buttons, flowers from proms and junior proms, a friendship ring from Timmy Rudolph, a little statue of the Virgin Mary.

She brings the shoe box to church, opens it up and the stuff rolls around. The statue slips from on top of the tiny baby and Isabel sees his little mouth open in shock. The statue has killed her little embryo. "I'm sorry," says the grocery store mom. "Would you like another cup of soup?"

*

On Easter, Isabel and Mark attend mass with her family. They are appropriately cloaked in light colors—khaki for him, seafoam for her. The Monteros fill up the center pew—her parents are at the end, close to the aisle. Millie and Mark are on either side of her, and baby Max, Frankie and Rachel are in the middle. During the sermon she makes faces not only at Max, but at the boy in the pew ahead of her and at the girl in a pink hat, two rows ahead of them. Every now and then Millie nudges her. "Pay attention would you?" she whispers.

But Isabel can't help it. She tries to listen to Father Jim as he stands in the pulpit talking about death, resurrection, et cetera, et cetera. He says something about the celebration of life and she dismisses him. Instead, she scours the church looking at the tiny babies and the small children all gussied up for Christ and Peter Rabbit. It's like window shopping, she thinks. She studies them as if they were little cars of different makes and models, of different years. Some are still coddled in baby fat and lace, bonnets and patent leather. Others stand on their own, with bottles caught in their mouths, stuffed animals trailing from their limbs. Then there are the ones who dress in black velvet and gold taffeta or dark blue sport coats and red ties. So many children, she thinks.

Max has on a sailor suit made of white cotton and trimmed in navy blue. His hair is dark and sticks straight up. When he smiles his dimples crease deep in his face and drool comes like a waterfall from his lush mouth. At communion, Frankie hands the baby to her and she lays him in her lap with his face looking right up at her. She runs her hands along his arms, his fat legs. "Dough boy," she whispers to him. "Dough boy, oh my little boy."

God did this to me, she thinks. Max giggles up at her as he sticks his fingers into her mouth, pulls the mask from the face of her heart. She leans over him, kisses his forehead, and when no one is looking she tells him, "You won't ever know this. Boys never do." She pulls him up by his tootsie-roll arms and leans her head on his. "It's the worst, Max," she tells him. "It hurts."

"Are you okay?" Frankie asks. He reaches down to pick the baby up from her. "You don't look so hot."

Now is the time, she thinks. Tell him now. He takes Max from her and balances him on his hip. He looks like he's babysitting, she thinks, not at all old enough to be a dad. "Oh me? I'm just weepy 'cause we're all here. That's all," she tells him. "I'm perfectly okay."

*

She has developed a taste for cup-of-soup. It's all she eats for lunch—maybe that and a bagel or toast. She tells the other teachers at work it's an inexpensive meal and filling too. She likes the way hot water brings the noodles to life, softens the freeze-dried vegetables, fills the tiny shrimp with breath.

Sometimes Mark stops in at school to take her out to lunch, but she never wants to leave the building. "I brought my lunch," she always tells him. "It's all I need. And besides, I don't like leaving my kids."

She calls them her kids—the second graders at Elmwood Elementary. They love her because she spends rainy lunch hours in the cafeteria gym, cranking tunes and dancing with them—the Running Man, Roger Rabbit, the Electric Slide, the Butterfly. They think she's cool and they don't hesitate to sit on her lap or hide behind her legs. Sometimes she even lets the girls braid her long black hair. She gives them nicknames like Bubba and

Queenie and Sista Snap and what she loves most is when they read to her, her kids, her babies, the second grade class at Elmwood Elementary.

Her kids think she's a kid. They want to see pictures of her mom and dad. They ask all about her brother. "Are you the boss of him?" they ask. "Is your sister Millie a baby still?" they want to know. They don't believe she has a boyfriend. Once Arnold Heskett said, "But you're too young to like boys." They never ask her if she's a mom. They know she isn't. They can tell from the way she plays and the way she talks about numbers and adding and subtracting. They can tell from the wild crayons and giant colored chalk on her desk.

At the end of the day, she arrives home exhausted, so tired that while Mark makes them dinner, she naps.

*

He reaches for Isabel in the dark, draws her to him, and still, lying there she feels completely alone. Turning to face him, she says, "I wish you could know this."

"I've tried," he tells her. "But this has really wigged you out— who are you anyway? Don't you remember how upset you were when you found out you were pregnant?"

"I wasn't upset." She turns to face the window, looks at the blue fingernail of the moon. The curtains shimmy in the light, and it's as if spring were breathing onto their bed. "I was surprised."

"You never wanted a baby before, Bella. What is this? I don't think I can take too much more."

He'll never get it, she thinks, how it feels to have this little bit inside you wilting like the petals of a flower, slipping out of you like rot. As if the seasons have skipped around—spring to winter, no in-between. Everything upside downside up.

"What, you mean you'll leave me? I thought you loved me," she tells him. He throws his hands up in the air and lets her slip out of his arms. She rolls to the very edge of the bed, curls her legs up to her chest, and dreams of soup and cereal shaped like little lifeboats floating in a sea of milk. The moon engages the dance of lights, balances little white flames against the sky. The rain is falling fast, pelting down on the house and Isabel swims to shore. Her arms move like giant windmills—slow motioned and circular—her legs kicking at nothing like running on the weightless moon. She dreams her baby awake.

HER WILD AMERICAN SELF

It's like my family's stuck somewhere on the Philippine Islands. My grandmother, *Lola* Mona, says that I'm as wild as *Tita* Augustina. That I have that same look in my eye. A stubbornness. And if I'm not careful I will be more trouble than she ever was. She says her daughter was a hard-headed *Americana* who never learned how to obey, never listened. Like me, she says. My family believes that telling her story will act as some kind of warning, that I might learn from her mistakes.

When she was young, Augustina wanted to be chosen. Maybe it was all those movies about Teresa and Bernadette, flying off to heaven, but she imagined she would be a modern-day saint from Chicago's North Side. Sitting at her window before bedtime, she'd divide the night into decades and mysteries. The moon was a candle offering and she surrendered prayers to Mary by that light.

When she was eleven, Augustina wanted to be an altar girl. In a red robe and white gown, she dreamed of carrying the crucifix down the aisle. Her mother wouldn't hear of it. "God loves your devotion, *hija*," she'd say. "He loves you whether or not you carry Him down the aisle at church."

To rebel, Augustina stopped going to Mass with the family.

"God loves me," she'd tell her mom. "Whether or not I show up on Sundays."

Augustina's dad, Ricardo, clenched his jaw tight, spitting words through the space of his gold-capped teeth. "How can you do this to your mother?" he demanded. He gestured a bony brown finger at his wife who was collapsed on the living room sofa sobbing.

"How will this look?" she cried. "My own daughter missing Sunday Mass. People will talk."

Augustina tried bargaining with them. "Let me be an altar girl, let me keep playing baseball with the neighborhood kids and I'll keep going."

Mona let out a little scream. "Even worse!" she said. "Your reputation, *anak!*" Mona dramatically curled her palm into a tight little fist, and pounded her chest, keeping time with the painful beat of her heart.

Ricardo placed Augustina into the back seat of the car, threatening to send her to the Philippines for lessons in obedience. The threats meant nothing to her. She sat in the car all during Mass, making faces at the people who'd stare into the windshield. Next Sunday, her parents let her stay home alone.

This did not sit well with the family. When Mona and Ricardo moved to America, they brought with them a trunk full of ideas—land of opportunity, home of democracy, and equality—but God forbid we should ever be like those Americans—loose, loud-mouthed, disrespectful children. Augustina was already acting wild, and stubborn, opinionated too. To tame her, they sent Augustina to all-girl Catholic schools.

On her first day at Holy Angels, she walked into the cafeteria with her cold lunch—a tupperware of leftover rice and fish. There was a long table of girls sitting near the window. Recognizing some of them from class that morning, Augustina walked over to a space at the end of the table and as she got nearer, their voices grew silent. She greeted the girls and they smiled at her, they nodded. "Mind if I sit here?" she asked. They stared at her as if

Mary Mother of God had swiped their voices. They just stared. Augustina sat with them anyway. Then Colleen Donahue said, "This school's getting cramped." She was talking to the girl across from her.

"Yeah," the girl answered. "What *is* that smell?"

"God," Colleen said. "It's like dead fish."

Augustina scanned the table—the girls were eating oranges and apples. Some sat with nothing in front of them. She was the only one with a tupperware of food. Then she said to the girl sitting next to her, "What kind of lipstick is that? It's wild." But the girl turned her back on Augustina as if Our Lady had plagued her.

"I think it's coming from her," said the girl as she held her nose.

Augustina looked down the row of milk-white faces, faces so pure and fresh, it was hard to tell if they were born that way, or if they'd simply scrubbed the color out of them. She looked down at her hands, at the red nail polish peeling, at her fingers stretched out stiff in front of her. She had never noticed how brown her skin was until then. She would never have a single girlfriend among them. In fact, they say that Augustina's only real friend was her cousin Gabriel.

When Augustina got home that first day, she begged her mother to let her transfer to the neighborhood school, but her mother wouldn't listen. Instead she sat Augustina down on her bed, brushing the hair from out of her face and told her, "Your father and I work very hard to keep you in that school. It's the best, *hija*," she told her. "You'll see."

So she started hanging out with her cousin Gabriel in places they'd find disturbing. We have pictures that Gabriel took of Augustina dancing among tombs and statues of beautiful women saints at Grace Cemetery. In many of the photos, her image is like a ghost's. There's the snow-covered hills and Augustina's shock of black hair, her elephant-leg hip-huggers, moccasin-fringed vests and midriff tops, the scarves that sailed from the top of her head, the loose beads and bangle earrings flipping in the wind. They say her cousin Gabriel was in love with her, that he was what made her wild.

Mona used to complain to her husband, "Why does she always have to go to that place? Play among those dead people? Maybe we should have sent her to public school after all, Ricardo, or maybe we should have encouraged her friendships with those children, those boys next door." Her father, a hardworking surgeon, denied there was anything wrong. "Nonsense," he'd say, "She's a girl and she should act like one."

*

One night, when Augustina was sixteen, she locked the door to her bedroom, hid away from everyone. Her room was a sanctuary where Gabriel's photos plastered the walls, a row of votive candles lined her window ledge, and post cards of Lourdes and Fatima decorated her bedpost. She had built an altar of rocks from the beach up on Montrose, a tiny indoor grotto where she burned incense. She put on an old forty-five. Years later, Augustina would sing that song—about Mother Mary and troubled times and letting it go, or was that *be*? whatever—at parties and weddings and funerals and any event where she could bring her twelve-string guitar.

Lighting a cigarette, Augustina waved a match into the air. Then she slipped a hand underneath her pillow, pulling out a fine silver chain. At the end of the chain was a small medallion, oval like a misshapen moon and blue like the sky. From the center of the pendant rose a statue of the Virgin Mary, intricate and smooth like an ivory cameo. Augustina had taken the necklace out of her mother's jewelry box and kept it for herself. She believed it was her lucky charm.

She held the necklace between her fingers, rubbing its coolness into her skin, begging the Virgin to hear her. You were young, she whispered. You know what it's like to love a boy. She imagined her mother's swollen heart bursting and water spilling out, cascading down her tired body, mourning as though her daughter were dead. She'd never forgive her. After all the trouble her parents went through to keep her away from the bad crowd, the boys, and lust in general, Augustina still managed to fall in love. Her mom stood at the door, knocking loudly, but Augustina pretended not to hear. She took another drag of her cigarette, then snuffed it out in the cradle of a votive candle. Reaching to the side of the table, she lit a stick of incense, disguised the smoke with the scent of roses. She slipped the pendant under her pillow and held a picture of her sitting on the rocks at Montrose Harbor. She was wrapped in the cave of Gabriel's chest, curling her body tightly into his. The waves were high and one could see a spray of water falling onto them. Her mother would die if she saw that picture. "Augustina," her mother said. "Open up, *hija*, I want to know what's bothering you."

"Nothing, Mama," she answered. "I'm just tired."

Her mother jiggled the door. "Open up. Let me look at you, you were pale at dinner." She waited another moment and then asked, "Why don't you talk to me, Ina? Let me know what's wrong."

Talking to her mother was like talking to the house plants. With good intentions, she would sit, gladly nodding, smiling, but she wouldn't hear. Like the time Augustina tried to tell her mother about the nuns, how they pointed her out in class, saying things like, "Thanks be to God, Augustina, the Church risked life and limb to save your people, civilize them. Thank God, there were the Spanish and later the Americans." All her mother said was, "She meant well, *hija*. Try to be more patient."

*

The next morning Sister Nora gave her annual lecture to the sophomore class. Standing against a screen, a giant projection of the world splattered across her face and the gym at large, she waved a long pointer in the air, gestured at the map. "There are cultures," she said, "that go to great lengths to keep their daughters chaste." Augustina envisioned a large needle and thread stitching its way around the world, gathering young girls' innocence into the caves of their bodies, holding it there like the stuffing in a Thanksgiving turkey. She had to excuse herself.

The heat in the building was too much, too suffocating. Every time she closed her eyes she saw her mother's image on the screen before her or she'd picture the girls in South Africa, their stitches bursting wide open. Augustina ran out. She sat on the curb, cupping her hands against the wind, her thin legs sprawled out in front of her. She slipped a cigarette between her lips and listened to the girls' voices wafting out of the building. She hated everyone at that school.

A low riding vehicle, brown and rusted, snaked its way along Holy Angel's driveway. Augustina took another drag from her cigarette. As she rose and moved away from them, she could hear the girls howling.

"It's her sexy cousin," yelled one girl. "The Filipino house boy."

"You'll get caught," Colleen said plainly.

As she climbed into Gabriel's Mustang, Augustina swore under her breath, asked, "Yeah, so what's it to you?"

*

He drove uptown, taking side streets, weaving the car about pedestrians. His camera, a thirty-five millimeter he had inherited from his grandfather, was carefully placed next to him on the seat. It was his *lolo*'s first possession in the States. Reaching for it, Augustina played with the zoom, slipping it back and forth, in and out like a toy.

"Don't break that," Gabriel warned.

The light from outside framed his profile. She could see the angle of his cheekbones, how they jut from his face, the slope of his nose and the dimples that were set in his half-smile. She snapped a picture of him, click, rewind, click. Snapped another. She pointed the camera out the window and watched the streets through an orange filter. They rode most of the way in silence and then he finally said, "So did you think about it?"

"Yep," she sighed, "it's all I can think about."

"Me too," he said.

"Maybe we should stop hanging out so much," she said. "Maybe that would help."

But Gabriel shook his head. "That's not right either."

The window was splattered with slush from the streets. Through the view finder, she caught a girl carrying a baby. The infant, dressed in a light blue snowsuit, draped its body across the girl, curled its head into the crook of her neck, slept comfortably amid the winter traffic. Click, she snapped another picture.

Augustina thought the girl carrying the child looked like Emmy Nolando, the daughter of her parents' tennis partners. Apparently, Dr. Nolando refused to give his daughter birth control and when she came home pregnant, the Nolandos sent her to a foster home in town. Disowned her. Augustina's parents milked the story for almost an entire year:

"Can you imagine," her mother whispered as she leaned over her bowl of soup. "The shame of it."

When Augustina asked why Emmy was sent away, her father shook his head, and muttered, "Disgraceful."

Ricardo leapt into a long lecture concerning those loose American girls and their immorality. "She's lucky she's not in the Philippines," he said. "There she'd have that baby and her parents would raise that child as their own."

"That's stupid," Augustina said.

"Oh yes," Mona said. "That baby would never know who his real mommy was. That's how it's done back home. That's how they save the family's reputation."

Even though Emmy had spent her pregnancy in a foster home, and even though she gave her baby up for adoption, Augustina was still told not to speak to Emmy. No one did. The Filipino community ignored her. "Better not be wild, better not embarrass the family like that girl. Better not, better not, better not."

*

Of all their hangouts, Grace Cemetery was their favorite. At Grace, the sun shattered into a thousand bright icicles, splintering branches into shadows, casting intricate patterns on hills of white. New fallen snow draped the statues of saints and beautiful ladies like white linen robes. They stood at the doors of these tombs and they prayed for souls. They stood guard no matter what—storms or drought. Once a twister ripped across Grace Cemetery and trees broke in half—a couple of tombstones even uprooted. But these women stood strong.

She sat at the foot of St. Bernadette's statue, gathering snow into little heaps. When Bernadette was visited by the Blessed Virgin back in Lourdes, they thought she was crazy. They didn't believe her. But Bernadette didn't give a fuck what they thought. She just kept going up that hill, praying, talking to Holy Mary like it was nobody's business. Augustina ran her hands along the statue's feet, tracing the finely etched toes with the edge of her finger. She listened to the wind winding its voice through the trees like a cool blue ribbon.

Gabriel fiddled with his camera, flipping through filters and lenses. She watched him sitting on a hill, his long body bent over the camera, his hair falling to either side of his face, shining midnight under the hot winter sun. Augustina believed Gabriel was an angel in another life. She could tell by his pictures, black and white photos of the city and its people. He once told her that truth cannot possibly hide in black and white the way it does in color. Colors distort truth, make the ugly something beautiful. She considered him brilliant.

"Bless Gabriel," she told the statue. Augustina looked up at the saint's full cheeks which were round and smooth like the sun. Her eyes were carved into perfectly shaped hazelnuts—so lifelike that from here Augustina could see the definition of her eyelashes.

"Augustina!" Gabriel yelled. "Look up." He jumped up onto someone's tombstone. The light from behind him glared at Augustina, forming a haze of white around his black mane. "This light's great," he said. "Your eyes are magnificent."

"I'm squinting," she said. He leapt from the side of the tomb, and leaning over her, he tugged at the ends of her hair.

Augustina placed a cold hand on the side of his face and he shivered. "What would your parents say," she asked. "What would we do?"

He stared at the graves. The sun slipped behind a crowd of clouds and suddenly it was cold out. Augustina lit a cigarette and offered him a drag. He buried his face in his hands as he pushed her away.

Getting up, she slipped away, walked underneath the rocks that formed an archway where Mary stood serenely veiled in paint—skyblue and gold. Tossing her cigarette to the ground, Augustina walked past the bench, pushed up against the iron rail, leaned her pelvis into the gate and pulled at one of the rods. She stared at the thick wooden rosary that draped Mary's white hands. Augustina told the Lady, "It feels natural. Why not?"

She had not meant for any of it to happen. A few weeks before, *The Chicago Tribune* awarded ten prizes to the best high school photographers. A manila envelope came to Gabriel's house thick with a piece of cardboard, his prize winning photo of the Rastafari woman on Maxwell Street, and a check for two hundred dollars. Second prize. The letter that came with the announcement talked about Gabriel's use of light, texture and composition. The judge said Gabriel's intuitive eye was not only a gift but a way to see the world. Gabriel should develop his potential.

When Gabriel showed his father the letter and winning photo, Uncle Hector blew up. Told Gabriel he was wasting his time again, taking risks with his life, travelling into dangerous neighborhoods and for what? A picture? "Don't be stupid," Hector told him. What if something would have happened there on the Southside? He could have been mugged or knifed or beaten. He could have been shot from the gun of a passing car. Was he crazy, Hector wanted to know. Grabbing Gabriel's camera, Hector shook it over his head like a preacher with a Bible, its strap casting shadows on his face. "Enough of this," he said. "Stop wasting your time." As he threw the camera across the kitchen, the lens popped open, came crashing on *Tita* Belina's marble floors and shattered.

That night, Augustina had sat on the rocks at Montrose Harbor, holding Gabriel's head on her lap, brushing the hair from his face, wiping the tears as they rolled from the corners of his eyes. "Count the stars," Augustina whispered. "Forget him." Augustina felt so bad for him, so angry at her uncle. And when Gabriel glanced up at her, she leaned down to meet him and kissed. She let her lips rest there, held onto him, and something in her stirred, some feeling she was not accustomed to. She let go a long sigh, let go that little bit of loneliness.

*

Augustina thought she saw the Lady smiling at her, looking right through her. Okay, she whispered, I can't stop thinking about him. Am I bad? At night she imagined the weight of his body pushing down on her, covering her like a giant quilt. She saw his eyes slipping into her, his beautiful face washing over her in the dark. She tried to remember the feel of his hair, how the strands came together, locked around each other. Sometimes she thought she could smell the scent of him, there at the lake, a fragrance of sandalwood, a breeze from Lake Michigan. I'm crazy, okay, she thought. A tramp, if you will. But he loves me, Mary, doesn't that count?

She thought of Sister Nora and the girls whose parents made sure of their virginity. How they'd mutilate them in the name of chastity. And does that operation keep those girls from love, she wondered. Does it keep them from wanting him? Sister Nora would find out and tell everyone. Use her for an example. No, she'd rather die. She imagined her body floating, swelling in the depth of the lake. She imagined herself swimming eternally. Augustina closed her eyes, putting her face to the sky. The sun came out every few seconds, ducking out of the clouds so that

Blessed Virgin Mary appeared hazy and kind of aglow—but only for seconds at a time. "Hail Mary," she said. "Hail Mary full of grace, the Lord is with thee, so please, please, please, put in a word for me, Hail Mary." She was so deep in prayer, she didn't even hear Gabriel sneak up behind her.

"Are you worried?" Gabriel asked.

"A little." she said. He put his arm around her and they embraced. Kissed. Slowly fell into that long black funnel, slipping across borders they had never crossed till now. They spent the rest of the day lying under the branches of the grotto, watching the changing sky and waiting for the sun to sleep. Neither one of them wanted to go home.

*

The house was locked when she got there, so Augustina fumbled for the key she wore around her neck. When she opened the door, the symphony from her father's speakers rushed out to her like waves on Montrose beach. Music filled the house so that when she called out to her mother, her voice was lost and small.

Mona stood at the stove, her feet planted firmly apart, one hand on her hip and the other stirring vegetables. Augustina snuck up behind her and kissed her softly on the cheek. "Hi, Mommy," she whispered. Mona continued to mix the stir fry, beating the sides of the frying pan with quick movements. Beads of sweat formed at her temples as she worked. "Do you want me to set the table?" Augustina asked. Turning, she saw the table was already set. Four large plates, a spoon and fork at each setting, a napkin, a water glass. "Okay," Augustina sang. "Well maybe I'll wash up and I'll help you put the food out."

The music was blasting in her father's room. She popped her head in and waved at him. "Hi, Dad!" she called. He was reading the paper and when he didn't look up she tapped him on the knee. Leaning over, she kissed him.

"Sweetheart," he said. "Is dinner almost ready?"

"Yeah, Dad. In a minute."

She felt as though she had been up all night. Her body ached, was covered with dirt from the cemetery. Gabriel's cologne had seeped into her skin, and she was afraid that her mother had sensed it. So instead of simply washing her hands, she bathed.

The cool water, rushing down her body, washed away the cigarette smoke, the cologne, the dirt. She could almost feel the water coursing through her, washing over her mind, cleaning out her tummy, circling about her heart.

When she got back to the kitchen, she found she was too late. Her mother had placed a huge bowl of rice on the table, a plate of beef and vegetables and a tureen of soup. "Sorry, Ma," she said, as she grabbed a cold pitcher of water. "I just needed a shower."

"Is that all, Augustina?" her mother asked as she looked up from the sink. "What did you do today? Ha? Where were you?"

She felt her face burning bright red. "At school," she answered, "Where else? Then Gabriel and I went to the mall."

"School?" she whispered. "They were looking for you at school." Augustina stared at the table, ran her fingers around the edge of the water pitcher. It was cold and moisture shivered from the pitcher's mouth and ran down its sides. Her mother's voice was low and angry. "How many times do we have to go through this, *hija*? Why can't you just stay in school?"

"But I was feeling sick," Augustina said.

"So you had Gabriel pick you up and the both of you were absent?" Her mother threw a dish rag on the counter. "You were at the cemetery again?" She pulled Augustina close to her. "Do you want your father to send you to the Philippines? Maybe that would teach you how to behave." Her parents often threatened to send her there, to all-girl convent schools, where nuns pretended to be mothers. "If you think the rules are strict here, wait till you have to live there."

"Sorry, Mom," Augustina whispered. "But the truth is that Gabriel had another fight with Uncle Hector and he was upset. He came to get me so we could talk."

"Still, *hija*, that's no reason to be absent from school." As

Mona brushed the hair out of her face, and kissed the top or her forehead, Augustina's father stepped into the kitchen.

"*Ano ba*," he asked. "What's going on?"

Mona tucked her hair behind her ears and told him, "Nothing, nothing, Ricardo. Dinner is ready. Come sit. Ina, call your brother."

*

Augustina spent the next two days locked up in her room, blasting her record. The needle slipped over that old forty-five, bumped along the grooves and scratches, whispering a mantra. "Mother Mary," she sang along. "Comes to me." An old church organ cranked a sacrilegious funk, a honky tonk, that seemed to fade into the slow rise of the electric guitar's bridge. She played around with Gabriel's photos. She mounted them on cardboard and painted borders around them—daisies and rainbows and splotches of love and peace and kiss drawn in giant bubble letters. Her mother stood at the door, knocking, forever knocking, but she pretended not to hear. "I'm not feeling well," she had told her mother. "I don't want to go to school." Bile rose up her throat, churned in her stomach, swamped up against the cavern in her chest.

Her family came to the door one by one. First her mother, then Dad. Even Auntie Belina, her cousin Ofelia and Uncle Hector came knocking, but the door was locked and there was no opening it. When Gabriel stood at the door, she whispered through a crack, "I'm sorry, I can't let you in. They can't know."

When Augustina finally went to school, Sister Nora stood in front of the classroom, whacking her giant pointer stick across the blackboard. "There has been disgraceful conduct. Sin, sin, sin. Apparently, the story of the young girls and their experience with genital mutilation has not taught you anything. You girls must be punished."

Augustina thought the nun knew, was about to expose her when Sister ordered the girls who attended Kat O'Donel's slumber party to step forward. Apparently the sisters found a video

tape of "Marlin the Magnificent" dancing in his elephant mask—
and that was all he wore—a mask. The tape was found lying in
the Cathedral—second to the last pew, across from the confes-
sional. Fran Guncheon, class librarian, and Augustina were the
only ones not in attendance, so they were given permission to
leave. Augustina took this opportunity to run to Grace cemetery.

*

The clouds drifted north, slipped by fast like the second hand in
her grandmother's wristwatch. Her body was numb, frozen like
the Ladies in the court. She thought they had grown sad. Her
constellation of saints, like everyone else in her life, had stopped
listening to her. Snow melted around St. Bernadette; the sun
burned holes in the ice underneath her. Augustina smelled the
earth, seeping through the slush. It was sweet and fertile. A trick-
le, a tear, maybe the melting snow, slipped down Bernadette's
face. Inside Augustina, something grumbled, roared. She had
stopped praying weeks ago. God confused her.

Augustina looked up from the statue and saw her mother
climbing over the hill. The sun shrouded her in light. She wore
her off-white cashmere coat, the one that fell to her ankles
because she was so short. She wrapped her black hair in a white
chiffon scarf that trailed past her shoulders, followed the wind.
There was a cloud of white smoke trailing from her breath, rising
up and floating away from her. When she came near, her mother
said, "She's beautiful."

"She's strong," Augustina answered.

"So this is where you go." She tugged at Augustina's braids,
examined her face, kissed the top of her forehead. Then, pulling
the chain from Augustina's neck, she said, "Where did you get
this, *hija*?"

"Isn't it my baby necklace? I found it in your jewelry box."

Her mother shook her head. "I got this from my godmother.
You shouldn't have taken it without asking."

Slipping her head onto her mother's shoulder, Augustina felt her body soften, the energy draining from her. She considered telling her mom about Gabriel. Would she understand? She closed her eyes and fell in time to her mother's breathing. Maybe, she thought. Her mother embraced her and told her, "Whatever is troubling you, *hija*, don't worry. Family is family."

*

Of course, *Lola* Mona never tells me that part of it. The story goes that *Tita* Augustina went to the Philippines six months later. Some of the relatives say it was to have a baby, others say it was to discipline her wild American self. Still stuck back on the islands, they tell me, "You're next. Watch out." Even my mother thinks her older sister was a bad girl.

"How do you know?" I ask her. "You weren't even born when she left. You hardly knew her." My mother always shrugs her shoulders, says she just knows.

Last time I went to see *Tita* Ina, she held out her tiny fist, wrinkled and lined with blue veins, and slipped me the Blessed Virgin dangling from the end of a fine silver chain. "Here, *hija*," she said, "take this." I placed the necklace up to the light. The paint was fading and chipping from it's sky blue center, but still there was something about Her. The way Her skirts seemed to flow, the way Her body was sculpted into miniature curves, the way the tiny rosary was etched onto the metal plate.

LECTURES ON HOW YOU NEVER LIVED BACK HOME

You grew up hearing two languages—one you can pull apart, name, slap a series of rules to, twist like clay-dough in a child's hand—the other you cannot explain, you listen and you know. It is a language you understand intuitively—like being able to read the sunrise, the strips of pink and orange, the clumps of uneven clouds, a thin patch of grey and the moon and somehow, without thinking twice, you know what kind of day it will be. You understand like this because you are the first born. First generation. First American. First cousin. First hope.

Back home, one of your grandmothers sewed children's clothing by hand and sold them in an open-air market. The other grandmother raised seven children on her own, gathering them up, hiding them away in the provinces along the sea, away from Japanese soldiers, away from American fighters. Away from war. Your grandmother feared the safety of all her children, especially her young ladies. Your mother survived wartime. She was smart and well-read and ambitious, skipped grades, travelled across the oceans, met your father in Milwaukee, gave up her princess status to be your mother. As a boy, your dad farmed fish out of monsoon-swollen rice paddies, cut school to hitchhike from Pampanga to Rizal just to see MacArthur. Somewhere in his youth, he spied on American GIS and caught on to this notion of democracy, this notion of rights. His rights, his family's rights, the rights of his countrymen. The rights taken first by three hundred years of Spanish rule, then Japanese terror and war, then of course, there were the Americans and their intentions. After sneaking about soldier camps, making friends with a GI from Atlanta, bumming cigarettes from another one from Pasadena, your father worked his way out of those provinces, studied hard at school. He passed his boards, passed immigration, slipped into that ballroom on Racine and Wisconsin, and charmed his way into your mother's life.

They raised you to understand that back home, a young girl serves her parents, lives to please them, fetches her father's slippers and her mother's cups of tea. Back home a young girl learns to embroider fine stitches, learns parlor dances, wears white uniforms at all-girl schools, convent schools. She never crosses her legs or wears skirts above the knee. Back home a girl does not date. She is courted. And when there is a young man present, there is always a chaperon. Young ladies grow up to be young housewives, good mothers, and in their old age, they still behave like obedient daughters.

You, on the other hand, have never had to obey a curfew because of war, never had to tiptoe through your own house, never had to read your books underneath a blanket where no soldier would see. As far as you knew, your curfew was your curfew because Mom and Dad said so. You were raised in suburbia in a split-level house, always in fashion, even when you were only two, dressed in your white lace and pink ribbons, toting your very own parasol. You've never been without heat, without food, without parents. All your life your worries consisted of boys and pimples and overdue books. You had your first boy-girl party when you were five years old, played Pin-the-Tail-on-the-Donkey and kissed Timmy Matasaki underneath the dining room table. You had a bad habit of talking back. You learned how to scream no to your parents, and it didn't matter if you were punished, slapped across the face, sent away to sulk, banished to the kitchen, you still opened your mouth and the words came out.

You grew up pouring chicken soy sauce dishes over beds of steamed rice, never mashing potatoes until you were on your own, eating your meals with a spoon in your right hand, a fork in the left, marvelling at the Americans and how they could balance entire meals on one fork, or the Chinese who could eat bowls of rice with two sticks. Your family roasted pigs on a spit, while next door, the neighbors cooked brats and burgers on electric grills.

From the start, you were a piece that did not fit, never given the chance to be like the rest—the ones with blond hair and red hair and something someone called strawberry. The ones with eyes that change like the ocean—green to blue to seafoam, depending on the color of their sweater. Your eyes have always been black. Your hair dark. Straight. No variety. To the kids at school, you were no different from the other Oriental girl, the one who spoke English with a chopped-up accent. To your aunts and uncles you were turning into a *bratty Americana*, loose like those blond children, mouthy like the kids who ran the streets wild. They worried you might grow up too indelicate for marriage.

Now you are well over twenty-five and still single. The old aunts raise one eyebrow and say, See? But you know, it's because you refuse to settle for less than best. Anyone can get married, you say. You not only tell men off, you ask them out. Recently, you've considered having a child without a father. This attitude bangs up against your mother's heart like the bumpers of two cars when she's parallel parking and the car doesn't fit. Sometimes she looks at you and sighs.

Your home is in Bucktown, Wicker Park, Ravenswood, Illinois, and because you won't admit the fact that what your parents call "back home" has made a place in your house, because you are not white, and still you are not one of them—the foreigners—you continue to displease everyone. Your father's headache is mostly just you. He has been known to throw his hands up, call you stubborn, say *Bahala na!* It's up to you. Your choice. Your responsibility.

Still, in the privacy of your kitchen, you admit you cannot live without your family, your history, this ideal called "your people." You cannot divorce yourself from yourself. You know you are the hyphen in American-born. Your identity scrawls the length and breadth of the page, American-born-girl. American-born-Filipina. Because you have always had one foot planted in the Midwest, one foot floating on the islands, and your arms have stretched across the generations, barely kissing your father's province, your children's future, the dreams your mother has for you. Because you were meant for the better life, whatever that is, been told you mustn't forget where you come from, what others have done for you. Because all your life you've simply been told. Just told. Because a council of ancestors—including a few who are not yet dead, who are not even related to you—haunt you, you do your best. You try. You struggle. And somehow, when you stand in the center of a room, and the others look on, you find yourself acting out your role. Smart American girl, beautiful Filipina, dutiful daughter.

FIGURES

Ana Sandoval closed her eyes and imagined the bodyscape, round and full, dimpled and ripe. She liked creating delicious shapes, circular, free-flowing shapes. She had designed a series of nudes—fat men, newborns, tarts and naked cats, bowls of exposed fruit. None of the paintings looked like her subjects. Even a vase full of daffodils looked nothing like the original. Ana distorted the petals so that they'd hang full-lipped, so that the leaves on the window sills would bleed earth-green.

Today she worked on a self-portrait. She had begun the painting last spring, when she and Jeff first met. He would come over while she was working, with a bottle of wine, a video rental or Thai food—something—he always brought something over, distracting her from her work. At first this was okay, but he came over a lot and it seemed that for a year she was always distracted. They were always together. She never finished the painting.

She stood on a platform in the middle of her studio, completely naked. Three giant mirrors lay flat against a wall, reflecting her easel, a white canvas, an old-fashioned bathtub with four brass legs, and Ana. She wanted to define the shape of her body, but all she could see was a gathering of cellulite at the upper reaches of her thighs. Faint blue tributaries travelled the course of her legs like a map of Chicago leading west to the suburbs. Where prune-size bruises dressed her calves she imagined southern Illinois: Normal, or Centralia, or Cairo. The worst were her breasts. They wobbled like depleted little water balloons left out too long, forgotten. Her upper arms lay flat, unable to identify muscle, shape, and tone. Even though her complexion was the color of espresso, she painted it a yellow-beige from the tube marked "Flesh." At least I have a nice smile, she thought grinning at her reflection, and dimples. She turned her back to the mirror and hummed, lots and lots of dimples. Ana ran her hands through her thick black hair which was cropped short and stood high up on its ends. She squinted at herself and sighed. "This is never going to work," she whispered. She stepped into the bathtub, pulled out her lipstick and outlined her mouth in a dark red. "Hopeless," she muttered.

She climbed out of the tub and walked over to her paintings, examined a portrait of Jeff. Running her hands along the edge of the oils, she felt where the paint thickened at the chest and sloped into the waist, careened into the tendons of his thigh. She had exaggerated his jaw bones and the cleft of his chin, made his eyes a little darker than they were. Staring at his face, she flinched, felt a sting in her chest. "Jerk," she said out loud. She turned her attention to a portrait of her sister who lived in Seattle and her newborn niece, Sabina. Addy's dark breasts were still full of baby milk. Ana had painted them in such a way that each breast was as round and full as Sabina's head.

Ana's mother loved that new baby. Was always talking about her. Rita made it a habit to call her at least once a week to tell her how much she liked being a grandmother, a *lola*. "I'm glad you enjoy it," Ana would say.

"Too bad Addy lives so far away. Too bad I can't watch that baby growing up," her mother would continue. Sometimes Ana advised Rita to move. "Go out there," she'd say. "You can be with them." Once when really irritated, Ana told her mother she would have her own baby, no daddy, just the baby. That was not the answer her mom was looking for. Addy seemed so far away from Ana, her lifestyle a world away. In the portrait, mother and child were voluptuous like Lady Madonna and one of those ruby cherubs. The fact was, all Ana's portraits were voluptuous.

The phone rang and when she picked it up she could hear Hildy screaming over a dozen or so voices, over clinking glassware.

"Hey," Hildy screamed. "Get your butt over here. Where are you?"

She listened to what she imagined was a bus boy thrashing silverware into a plastic tray. Since Jeff left, Hildy called Ana every Friday, nagging.

"I want you to meet someone. He's a painter too—like you. Hot. Hot. Hot."

Ana ran her hands up and down the chord of her phone, twisted her fingers in the telephone wires. *Indigo, cobalt, vermilion,* she thought to herself. Hildy was like her mother, only younger. They were always trying to get her married off. Domesticated.

*

She met them at the Clay Cactus in Lincoln Park. Hildy, an old college friend of Ana's, loved Friday afternoon happy hours, tacky yuppie bars and traders. On this particular Friday, Hildy brought everyone together to this Mexican papaya cactus place for a two hour wait. The hostess walked up and down the waiting line with nachos and salsa and little shot glasses of red wine—on the house. They drank triple-sized margaritas amid recorded tapes of castanets and singing caballeros. The concrete terrace was flooded with hot sun which glared off the pink and green umbrellas of the Santa Fe lounge tables and chairs.

Ana showed up in a black cotton tank top that hung down past her ankles. She slicked her hair back so that it shimmered as though she had just gotten out of the shower. She wore no make-up and lots of silver bracelets.

"I love this place," Hildy told Ana. "Festive. I like that, don't you, Andre?"

Andre was the other painter. The rest of the group consisted of lawyers, brokers and traders. Blond ringlets sprouted from the top of his head like water from a suburban sprinkler. He had on Coke bottle sun glasses the color of rose petals with lenses that were as tiny as dimes. Hildy sat Ana in between Andre and her cousin, Harold.

Andre said, "Love this joint, Hildy, really love it." Then he smiled at Ana like he was pulling one over on Hildy.

"It's overdone," Ana told them. "Everybody's got Santa Fe. Even Mac's down the street's doing Santa Fe."

"Now there's a place that doesn't have a two-hour wait," Harold suggested. "Mac's."

"You could have all this," Ana said, gesturing to the patio, "and still eat in less time than it would take to get a table here." She hated waiting.

"Ugh," crooned Andre, "But just think of the food ... so not healthful."

"Give me a neighborhood dive. An Elvis bar. A pool hall," Ana went on. They sat with a lazy susan. Harold spun the wheel with his finger, watching the baskets of nachos and bowls of salsa as they rotated past.

"Yeah, I hate these places, Hildy," Harold said. "Why are you always the one that picks these awful bars?" Harold kissed Hildy's rouged cheek, then loosened his tie and shook off his summer suitcoat. Ana noticed the dirt marks at his collar, imprints of the human condition. Here, she thought, is the aftermath of a man who's forced to dress in starched shirts and three-piece suits and then made to ride public transportation at a hundred and one degrees. His hair was too long for the suit, which made her think he must be good at whatever he did since they let him keep his hair.

"So," Harold said to Ana. "You're a painter? Houses or what?"

"Kitchens," she laughed. "Actually, for money I'm a fragrance model and then I paint nudes."

"Women or men?" he asked grinning.

"My god," Hildy laughed. "She'd paint her own mother naked if she could."

Then he wanted to know, "What the hell's a fragrance model?"

"You know," Ana told him. "I squirt old ladies with *parfum* and then I give 'em samples." She earned twenty bucks an hour and all she had to do was walk around in high heels, lots of makeup and an outfit from Finer Dresses. "What do you do?" she asked Harold. Andre leaned his elbows on the table, leaned across Ana, as if he were absorbed in the conversation.

"I'm a broker."

"And what do you break, exactly?" she asked smiling.

"It's boring," Harold said. "Trust me, you don't want to know."

"No," Andre jumped in. "But tell us anyway."

Harold leaned towards Ana. "Some old lady pushed a guy off the 151 on Michigan and Erie," he whispered. "She made me nervous so I gave her my seat." Ana laughed. Andre pushed his chair back and sighed.

"City life scares me," Harold continued. Then he tugged on her silver bangles and whispered, "Let's say you and me climb these walls and head over to Mac's." After that Harold got up and left. Ana thought he was just going to the bathroom, but he had run down the street and brought back burgers and fries.

*

Harold could make her laugh. He wasn't her type, but he could make her laugh and this Ana liked. Since Jeff had professed undying love and left, Ana had not laughed at all. She knew that seeing Harold was only a diversion, a transition, while she recovered from the chest pains she suffered at night. Why, she wondered, does my heart actually ache?

On their first date, Harold walked Ana through the Lincoln Park Zoo and made faces at the seals that were lounging on the rocks near the aqua blue water hole. He took her hand and led her along the city beaches of Lake Michigan where they tiptoed around sun bathers and family picnics.

"Take your shoes off," she yelled to him against the wind.

"What?"

"Your shoes, take them off."

"No, I might step on a broken bottle, or a used condom. Besides," he said squeezing her hand, "I don't like getting sand in my shoes. But go ahead, you take yours off."

The lake waves, thunderous and rich, rolled in like giant scrolls of white paper. A harsh and angry wind spat sand at their bodies as they made their way south. They climbed from the rocks to cement piers and finally to the smooth city sidewalks.

"Take me to the Art Institute," he told her as they walked along Michigan Avenue. Their bodies smelled like children's bodies soaked in sun and playground. Still in shorts and T-shirts, windblown and dirty, they stepped into the museum and made their way along its cool corridors. "Teach me," he asked her. "What is the difference between Dali and Rubens and Monet?"

"Shut up," she laughed. "Don't make fun of me."

"No, Ana, really. I want to know."

Harold called Ana wondrous things. She told him he was full of shit, but she loved hearing him tell her how smart she was, how beautiful and strong she was. He said he knew all this before their first date, before the night was over at the Clay Cactus. Before Andre had snubbed his handshake on the way out.

Harold said he believed in her. She was talented. Gifted.

"But you've never seen my work," she told him.

"I can tell," he said.

Eventually the two found their way through a long black tunnel hallway, where they stood beneath the deep blue spell of Chagall's sapphire window and breathed.

*

He started bringing her presents—art supplies. Brushes, oils. He gave her a different tube of paint every week—cerulean blue, thalo green, viridian. Ana enjoyed Harold's company, but his compliments made her feel both flattered and uncomfortable. Jeff was supportive and sensitive, but too hip to jump up and down like Harold did. Now with Harold, she wasn't sure how to react—take everything with a grain of salt? Say thank you? Harold paid so much attention to the details of her life. Maybe, she thought, he'll mellow out. She hoped he would.

She teetered for a long time—friend, lover, friend, lover. She could take him or leave him. The only thing she knew was that he was a fine companion. Her parents would probably love him. Then slowly, she found herself watching him—the way he uncrossed his legs in the middle of intense conversations and leaned his elbows on the tops of her legs, the way he talked to strangers and made them feel as comfortable as long-time friends. She followed his eyes and the shadows of his dark lashes. Studied the way his dimples creased when he was telling a bad joke. She caught him staring at her and unlike their first few dates, she stopped looking away.

And when two weeks later, at the end of the night, Harold leaned to kiss her, not goodnight, but hello, she dissolved slowly, sinking down, letting her posture go, letting everything go. She let herself breathe and imagined herself in one of those British films where the woman, who has been holding back, has suddenly been swept from some French painter's pallet onto his oatmeal canvas. That night was a drapery of colors, prussian blues, thalo green, manganese, peppered with a rose madder that somehow deepened into a rich spray of alizarin crimsons, cadmium reds and flashes of cobalt. She feared she was falling in love.

After he purchased all eighty-four colors of paint, he moved into her loft. During the first few weeks he'd dance around the studio with arms stretched out. He ran laps around the loft. "You've turned this old warehouse into a home," he told her. "God, this is cool."

That was during the daytime. At night though, Harold paced the floors. Looked out the windows. Sometimes he sat up and watched the trains go by.

"What's the matter, Harold?" Ana asked him.

"You really think it's safe here? You do, don't you?"

She smiled at him as she rubbed his back. Kissed him softly on his bare shoulder.

"Maybe we should think about getting a security system put in—for when you're alone," he said.

She studied the crinkles at the corners of his eyes, the way he didn't look at her when he said these things, and Ana smiled.

*

One day when they were at an estate sale in Kenilworth, they stopped by Ana's parents' house. Alan and Rita Sandoval had been married and living in Kenilworth for the past thirty years. When Ana and Harold walked in, they found her parents snuggling under a blanket on the family room floor. Giggling. Ana was embarrassed, but Harold thought it was cool. Her parents continued laughing.

"That's exactly how it should be," he told her on the way home. "Thirty years and still going." He gestured with his long and slender hand as he talked, and Ana thought sometimes Harold resembled a child. His dark eyes would grow round and dappled with light and he would ask questions incessantly.

"My parents?" she laughed. "They're completely embarrassing."

Ana listened to the wheels whacking the pavement on the freeway. She felt bad that Harold was so clueless. If her parents knew about their relationship, they'd try to break them apart. *Lamp black, mars black, umber.* She held his hand and squeezed it. She lifted the face of his palm to her lips and kissed. She stared at the orange lights on the road. She squinted at them so they blurred and lost their definition.

"I bet your dad walks in the door every night and yells, 'Honey, I'm home'," Harold said.

"You think so?"

"Sure I do, that's what it's all about. Being able to walk in the door and shout, 'Honey, I'm home'."

They drove to the city in silence. Her parents were far from perfect, she thought. She remembered the fights she used to have with her dad. How he didn't like the way she stayed out all night, and how he thought her friends were too unruly. Now if they knew she and Harold were serious, she sensed, they wouldn't have been so hospitable.

*

Dressed in his navy pin-striped suit, newspaper under his arm, attaché swinging at his side, Harold readied himself for the Board of Trade while Ana kicked the sheets from her legs, rolled out of bed and painted.

"Are you working today?" he asked her.

"Later," she said pulling paint brushes from a tin can.

Harold walked over to Ana and wrapped his arms around her, pulling her night shirt up as he touched her. "If we got married," he said, kissing her face, "you wouldn't have to go to work at all. You could stay home and paint all day."

"So," Ana sighed, "people stop needing money once they get married."

"Ha-ha. I'd support us." His kisses slipped from her lips, onto her cheek and down the nape of her neck.

"Not good enough, Harry," she said. She toyed with the buttons of his white dress shirt. She didn't want to think about getting any more serious than they were. He talked about getting hitched more and more and this made her uncomfortable—as though he had spoken to her mother and that marrying Ana off was a group project. Everyone was in on it—Hildy, her sister Addy, her parents, even Jeff was in on it at one time.

"Think how happy your parents would be if we got married," he said. Now the kisses were working their way around her collar bone, dipping between her breasts. She dropped the canister of paint brushes and bristled at the thought of her parents.

"You gotta go to work," she told him. "And I have to work on my portrait. Go. Go already." She pried herself away from him and bent down to gather the brushes.

Since Harold had moved in, she was finding it harder to get the shapes the way she wanted them. She couldn't get her arms to flow from her shoulders into her torso and down around her hips and she couldn't picture the shape of her belly. She'd stare into the mirror for hours and then at the canvas—the lines would not move with her hands—it was as if the brush had a mind of its own. She had been stuck for months, and so she'd paint nudes of other people—people she remembered from the street or from the bus. Often she'd watch the women shopping at Bloomingdale's or Saks Fifth Avenue and their exaggerated features—the heightened arches of penciled-in eyebrows or the slope of a restructured nose. She studied the round butts and the carrot-shaped thighs of suburban women as they walked away from her and her basket of perfume samples. She'd remember these bodies and she'd render them at home—watermelon bodies, pear-shaped faces, luscious rose-petal lips. She saw these distortions in the shoppers, in the housewives and grannies that drifted past her, snubbing her vials of floral scents and promises.

Most of the time she walked around looking for victims and her mind would wander far from Michigan Avenue. Her eyes would follow shoppers out the door, to their cars and into their homes in the suburbs.

Ana hadn't anything against love. She liked being in love. She loved Harold. She thought of Amelia Earhart, how she waited until she was about thirty to marry her agent. And she had been reluctant to do even that. Earhart once said she never wanted anything all of the time.

*

Sometimes Addy would call her from Seattle, clanking dishes and screaming baby in the background, while Ana doodled on pads of paper.

"He sounds like a dream," Addy said.

"Or a nightmare," Ana replied. She looked around the loft, at the clutter that seemed to be growing like cancer. "This place is starting to look like a junk yard." She kicked at his brief case.

"Don't blow this," Addy said. "You always manage to blow things."

Ana rolled her eyes and sighed. The baby was screaming. "Don't you feed her?" she wanted to know. She told Addy the paint was drying on her pallet, she had to go. "Sounds like you have to go too," she said and she hung up.

*

That next Monday, Ana wandered around the store, bringing her samples to the most unexpected departments. She handed out perfume vials in housewares and at the card shop, hung around the candy shop and nibbled at the free samples, shuffled about the furniture department practically in tears. In between customers she mumbled to herself, "I'm doing the right thing. I'm doing the right thing. I am." Giving in to Harold and her parents seemed to be less work than fighting them. After all, they were living together anyway, so marriage seemed like no big deal. What did it matter? She loved him and isn't that what all the songs on the radio were about? Love is all you need, et cetera, et cetera? *Viridian, venetian, vermilion.* "I'm doing the right thing," she sang. "The right thing." Ana ran her hands along the living room sets, the bedroom pieces and she thought, matching sets. Gross. When she got to the department with carpet samples, she tripped over a rolled-up rug and dumped the tiny bottles of perfume across the floor as indelicately and haphazardly as a child tossing rice at a church wedding. *Rose madder, terra rosa, rose red.*

When they eloped, Harold insisted on buying a house. "It's too dangerous out here, Annabella. I worry when you're home alone. Besides, we need a real house now. A place we can walk into and yell, 'Honey, I'm home!'"

"Who says?" she wanted to know, and while she said it teasingly, she did want to know, who says they needed a house.

When Ana first told her parents of their plans, her mom said, "But *hija*, he's not Catholic. He's American." Ana bit her lip so hard, she could taste the salt from her own blood. *Naples yellow hue, flesh tone, zinc.* There was no making her mother happy. And while her parents disapproved of their mixed marriage, they still fed Harold as though he had saved their daughter from some horrible fate. "Get her out of that treehouse," Rita said one night. She heaped Harold's plate full of stir-fry pork.

Harold nodded and said, "I don't know, we've been talking about it, and Ana really loves the loft. We might just settle there."

Ana's fingers slipped, fumbled with the fork in her hand as she looked at him.

"After all," he continued, "what counts is that she's happy and doing what she wants to do, isn't it?"

Her father slapped Harold across the back and handed him a Stoli-gimlet. "Good for you, son, good for you," he said.

Ana rolled her eyes. "It's a conspiracy," she whispered under her breath. When her mother handed her the plate, saying, "Eat more, *hija*," Ana pushed the dish away, her mind rattling, *Olive, avocado, almond,* as if it were a song.

*

They weaved their bodies about the crowd, about the fumes of bus exhaust, about the heat that rose from the cement below them. They side-stepped flattened soda cans and paper cups, they got out of the way of plastic grocery bags that floated like tumbleweeds down the busy city street. Standing at the corner in a group of Saturday shoppers, Ana turned to him and said, "You know, I have a bed. A great big king-sized bed."

"I'm getting you the best, Annabella. The very best. A brass bed and a Sealy Posture-Pedic that'll last our whole life."

They went into little stores, plopping onto various mattresses. He'd dive on top of silvery blue ones, quilted white ones, mattresses with little pink flowers, He'd invite her to join him, but Ana was reluctant. Once or twice a salesperson urged her to try too. "Lie down, honey," an old Polish woman told her. "Test and see. It's big enough for the two of you." On Broadway and

Melrose, they found a Sealy Posture-Pedic displayed in a storefront window. Harold rolled around like an otter, pulling Ana down, and giggling. "This is it, Annabella, this is it. Doesn't it feel great?"

"Harold," she said, as she looked at the small crowd gathering outside the store, "this mattress feels like concrete." She slipped out of his embrace and ran her hands along the sides of the bed. The fabric felt cool and shiny. It was quilted and stitched with plastic thread. She pressed her hands flat onto the mattress's face, the corners. A synthetic tag inked in black guaranteed its form, and shape. Guaranteed the perfect contour to every body.

Harold tackled her back down and held her. "It's firm and that's what counts. It's the best, Annabella. All the consumer guides say so."

Ana searched Harold's face. Sometimes in certain light—usually late afternoon light, Harold wore shadows on his face like a mask. It was another, one she did not know. She had never noticed how susceptible Harold was to advertising, to what others said. She tried to talk him out of the mattress. Said she'd never be able to rest on this rock. Despite all this, the mattress was delivered to them that following Thursday.

*

The bed was the first piece Harold bought. Ana could live with a new bed. The next weekend he purchased a leather couch, and then a player piano and then a marble table for twelve, complete with Roman pillars. "Do the busts come next?" she asked. Because Harold wanted Ana to feel at home, they kept everything in the loft, adding one eclectic piece to their lives; one right after another.

"What's the matter, honey," Harold asked as he swept her into his arms and danced her around the room. "Don't you like this table? Now we can have Hildy and Billy and the gang over for dinners."

"Who's gonna cook?" she wanted to know.

She found it harder to work in the space. There was less and less of it every week. And when she'd bump her way around the new end table and a grandfather chime (that didn't work, but looked good), she swore she'd have a talk with Harold. A fight would feel good, she'd think. I'll start one. But every time he walked in with a new piece, his eyes round and watery like a toddler learning to walk, his intentions busting out of his limbs as he offered her his gift, she'd soften, say, "Thanks hon, it's lovely."

They spent so much time in that bed. On weekends they propped themselves up with pillows and had all their meals there. On weeknights, they retired early and watched the ten o'clock news from that bed.

Sometimes in the middle of the night, Ana got up and pulled a pad of paper from underneath the bed and sketched Harold peacefully wrapped in an array of white blankets and quilts. She worked on the shape of his legs, the curve of his thighs and the tiny arch between his bum and back. She drew thick arms, carved with strong tendons and muscles. She liked the way moonlight swamped the room and shaped her husband into some kind of Adonis. She liked the way her husband looked when he slept. Watching him made her want to capture him just so. In the morning, she realized that the drawings looked nothing like Harold. She had drawn him out of proportion. His legs were not so long, his back, not quite so chiseled. She missed the flanks of fat others called love handles. Harold never noticed that she couldn't get his body right, "I look good sleeping, Annabella. Pretty good, except, don't you think you made my nose a little large?"

*

At the end of the loft, she rummaged through her paint brushes, trying to reach back into the shelves where she kept her supplies, when the phone rang. She stood up to answer it and banged her head on a brass-framed mirror Harold had bought to hang in her studio for what he called ambience.

"Shit," she muttered as she rubbed the sore spot. She ran, half blind with pain, knocking into end tables and chairs, slipping on Harold's yuppie skateboard. She was breathless and irritated by the time she answered the phone.

"Took you long enough," Addy said. Ana could hear Addy's husband singing to Sabina in the background.

"I fell."

"You need to be more careful," Addy said.

"You mean we need to get rid of some of this junk—Harold's a maniac, he keeps buying stuff."

"When are you going to New York?" Addy wanted to know. Ana had found a seminar on nudes. It was called Bodies of Work: A Nude and Nakedness Exhibit.

"In a couple weeks. Why, you gonna come babysit Harold?" At first Harold didn't want her to go. He told her he wouldn't be able to get off work that week. It was his busy season. "Why go at all?" she had said to him. "I'm a big girl." The sisters chit-chatted for a bit, exchanged loving digs and finally Ana asked her sister, "Are you ever alone anymore?"

"Are you serious?"

"Well, doesn't it make you nuts? Every time you call, you've got those back-up singers making noise."

"No—well, I mean sometimes it gets frustrating, but that's part of family life, you know? We're always here."

She sighed, thought, I was afraid of that. "I just never realized how much time I need."

"Need?"

"To be alone."

*

Ana was getting pieces together for a neighborhood gallery when Harold asked her to attend a company dinner. He called at three in the afternoon and said she should be ready by six.

"This is not a good time for me, Harold." She held the phone on the crook of her shoulder and balanced several paintings in her arms.

"This is important, Annabella. If you love me, you'll do this."

"My show's important too, Harold. It opens in two days. I need to work, hon. Can't you go without me?"

Ana sat in the middle of the studio surrounded by a field of canvas. Her legs sprawled out in front of her as she jiggled her bare feet. The ends of her hair were spotted with blue and scarlet paint. She couldn't decide between one of her drawings of Harold in bed and the one of Jeff. It seems, she thought, I had a better handle on the shape and contour of Jeff's torso—but she liked the form of Harold's body mixed with the linens. Jeff was just sitting in an easy chair—a typical nude. She studied Jeff's portrait closely and thought of the night he had thrown a drop sheet over her and her work and yelled, "Gotcha!" He had crawled underneath, crawled right up to her ankles and started nibbling. He had looked up onto her easel and said, "It's the kind of thing that makes me crazy!"

Everything was good between them, until he had wanted to make the relationship serious. Until he talked about marriage and babies. "You're starting to sound like my mom," she had said to him. In a couple of weeks he left. She was alone and she told herself that next time, she'd handle things differently. "I sure did that," she said out loud.

She didn't hear Harold enter the house and when she saw him standing at the door, she jumped. "Ana," he said. "It's past five. You're not ready."

"Oh, hi honey, you're home? Is it that late?" She got up and went to kiss him, but he turned away from the room before she got to him. "Sorry," she called out after him.

She heard him on the phone, and when he came back into the room he was dressed in his sweat pants and an old T-shirt.

"Are you going to your boss's dressed like that, Harry?"

"I told him you weren't feeling well." Rubbing his hands together, he said, "So what's going on here? How can I help?"

He hovered over her, for what seemed like seventy-five years. She felt his hot breath, moistening the nape of her neck, slithering down her collar bone.

"Honey," she said as she turned to look up at him. She put her hands on his shoulders, and pushed him away. "You don't have to do this. I'm okay. How about you go to that dinner—can you go alone? Or if you want, I'll get dressed and come with you."

"That's okay. This is important. Let's stay home and do this." He leaned over and kissed her cheek. "My boss understands."

"But you lied to him, Harold. I'm not sick." His face scrunched up and grooves of lines furrowed along his forehead and in the corners of his eyes. His eyes were so brown. She let her hands run from his shoulders to his fingers, there she grabbed onto him and squeezed. "I mean, this is so sweet of you, Harold, but you shouldn't make my work more important than yours. You should go."

Somehow, she convinced him to dress and leave. She could hear him moving about in the bedroom, could tell when he had put his wing-tipped black shoes back on. And when his footsteps faded out of the house, slipped out the door, she felt the air around her lighten.

She folded her legs underneath her body, curled up into a ball and cried. *Cobalt. Cobalt blue, cobalt green, cobalt violet. Purple. I could leave*, she thought. *I could just go.* She could almost hear her mother saying, "You are not trying. You must try." Fine, she thought as she pounded the floors with her fists.

*

She left for New York on a Thursday and told Harold she'd be back sometime Monday. Ana wandered through the marble halls of the Metropolitan Art Museum, studying various bodies. Gigantic figures, sculptures done in bronze and clay and statues chiseled out of granite and malachite anchored the museum's white halls. Of course, there were other oil paintings and water colors, drawings and charcoals of famous stars and politicians without their clothing. She attended a seminar on Michelangelo's David—they conducted something of an autopsy on the work, comparing it to Venus and the Pieta. Ana considered the works representational, though she refused to admit that to anyone. She attended a performance artist's rendition of "The Emperor's New Clothes" and cried.

After lunch, Ana slipped down a hallway and entered a room draped in muslin. In the corner of the gallery were photographs of couples. She was drawn to the photos, sepia-toned lovers twisted together, intertwined like clay pieces. One body began and slipped into another, hooked itself to another like a giant puzzle piece. The photographer never shot the faces. The bodies rolled and you could see the texture of the muscles, where the bones jut out, connected or were padded delicately with flesh. The one that drew her was of a man and woman who both had long blond hair. The camera shot down onto an array of sheets that made Ana think of Harold in bed. The woman's hair, a blond curtain drawn about her face, allowed the audience to glimpse at her chin and the fullness of her mouth. He knelt over her, so that their bodies overlapped, and if it were not for the definition of their muscles, one would not be able to tell his leg from hers, the place where his torso began and hers ended. His strong back tensed up as he held his arms out, holding up her head as if in prayer.

"Like that one?" said a voice from behind Ana.

"It's beautiful," Ana said. She turned to meet the voice. A tall woman, slender, dressed in a black patent leather catsuit, smiled at her. "Hey," Ana said, "isn't that outfit hot?"

"Not too bad," she said. "I'm Geni." She had a halo of white blond hair teased in wisps about her face with roots as dark as Ana's hair.

"These are nice," Ana told her. "I like the way you use space— it's so roomy. Was this a real couple?"

"That's me and my ex," she said.

"Really? Those too?"

"That's the only one of us—the rest are friends and models. I only shoot couples. Style the bodies together like they're props."

Ana thought this was interesting, the way Geni always worked with two, arranging the bodies just so. "My portraits are kind of surreal," she told Geni, "usually big and round, like apples." She looked back up at the photos, how the bodies draped together, seamless and free. It's enough to make a girl want to cry, she thought.

*

Geni's photos stuck with Ana, long after the body convention, and when she returned home, Ana turned in her basket of perfume samples. She tried to spend her time concentrating on her paintings, on her self-portrait, but she was often so upset, the lines and colors of her canvas body would slip from her control— grow ripe in places meant for slender lines, and areas that required shading, depth and light, grew static, two-dimensional. The portrait went nowhere.

"I just need time," she told him. "I need some space." Ana cleaned out a storage room in the back and set up her easel. She locked herself in there and spent the days working on her paintings. She got lost in the curve of her pallet and the shadows her body cast on the afternoon walls. She obsessed over shades of gray and charcoal. The oils from the brush slipped between her fingernails and into the cracks of her skin. Beige and browns and midnight blue speckled and striped her hair paint-gray. She worked on the shape of space, on blending colors so they danced about her hips, featured her full thighs, her jagged elbows.

She'd work so late into the night, she'd fall asleep in the giant easy chair in the studio or she'd collapse on the couch, not wanting to bother him already fast asleep. She imagined them lying side by side, touching bone to bone, joint on joint, her spine to his stomach. They were a perfect fit. Breathing brought them closer together. She remembered them in tandem. All night long, in tandem. She remembered hearing the eternal tick of a clock and feeling palpitations. A heart other than her own beating against the wall of her breast or the small of her back. She remembered how Harold would wrap his arms around her, cup his palm around her breast. How he'd whisper into the nape of her neck and leave beads of his breath resting there. She imagined they were one of Geni's portraits. She tried to remember the last time they were together, was it the way she remembered it, or was this memory like those night-time drawings of Harold?

Finally, after two weeks of this, he brought her a bouquet of paint brushes, a giant-sized canvas—white as a snowstorm in Alaska—a dozen boxes of European chocolate and a thousand promises. "I don't know why you're doing this," he said. "But I wish you'd tell me."

"Can't," she told him.

He slipped into Ana's room, into her studio and called out to her, "It's coming along, Annabella. This picture looks like you—in the eyes."

"Still just images."

"No Ana," Harold said as she walked over to him. "The other stuff is so outrageous, but this face is yours. Something real about it."

"Too representational," she told him. "I'm starting to think that my voluptuous bodies are what make my paintings." He sat down underneath the light from a halogen lamp and shivered. Ana approached him and ran her hand along the side of his body to warm him.

"Have you noticed that except for Addy and Sabina, I always paint single portraits?"

"Yeah," he said. "It's what you do."

She tried to tell him about Geni's work. How it moved her and made her realize she loved him, she did. "That's not the problem," Ana said. "It's marriage." She felt the tendons in his arm, the shape of his muscle, a little softer than she remembered. "Do you remember that story about the emperor's new clothes? How the whole thing was a farce?"

"You mean that kid's story?" He didn't get it, she thought. "So, you can't be married to me because you're an artist?" he asked.

Why didn't he get it? She traced his sides with the tips of her fingers, kneading the fat where his love handles had grown. "This is all so uncomfortable," she whispered, kissing him.

He sighed and looking at her, his face seemed to break, to crack like shards of a shattered mirror. Bad luck. "Now don't do that," she told him. He made it so difficult for her. It would have been easier, had she not loved him.

They fell asleep, holding each other like Geni's photos. She dreamed they were part of a gallery, a body of work. Figures, waiting to be arranged. She dreamed they were out on the lawn of a beautiful suburban house. Staring onto the yard she watched the sunshine fade and moonlight sneak around a lamppost. It was so dark, so dim, she could no longer make out the dream. Shadows grew into spirits and half movements. *Red. Crimson red, alizarin red, cadmium red. Vermilion.* Sleep washed over her and the shapes in the lawn were pieces of her life, misshapen and out of proportion. Her unfinished portrait loomed out in front of her. She dreamed her tears wet the ground where they lay, muddied and stained her face as she struggled beneath Harold's heavy body. She could not tell the difference, was she asleep, was this real? She imagined their bodies were stretched out across the grass, shapeless, sad and dying.

OUR FATHERS

Tessa Villa carried a picture of her grandparents in a little hemp purse around her neck. Brown-toned and porous, scalloped at the edges, it seemed to defy the passing of time. She'd stare at the photo for hours, running her finger up and down her *lolo*'s face, rubbing the picture to life, wondering which eye was the blind one. He wore dark glasses. Her father, Danilo, told her it was because one eye didn't work. Tessa focused on the lenses, hoping to see beyond the black-brown tint. She was concentrating, hoping to see the eyes behind them.

"You'll burn a hole into that picture, Tessa," her father told her. "Go help Mommy set the table."

It was dusk and they were surrounded by almost night. In their house, they conserved energy because Daddy said so. There were pockets of light in their home, in the kitchen where Tessa's mom worked, in the family room above her father's easy chair and over their dinner table, there was light, golden and safe. Danilo was reading the paper, listening to the six o'clock news and his daughter at once.

"Why does he wear sun glasses?" Tessa touched *Lolo*'s face, imagining what it would be like to lift the glasses. He stood at attention in a suit woven of shiny silk threads. His tie was dark, like the pomade-greased flat top of his hair. And if she squinted just right, Tessa could see her father in *Lolo*, his cheek bones sticking out above a slender face, his eyes black and strong beneath the tinted glass. Everything about *Lolo*'s expression, everything about his posture was serious.

Close to him stood her *lola*, dressed in a fancy gown, long and stiff and covered with embroidered flowers. Along the dress gleamed little clusters of pearls, like tiny bunches of grapes, opalescent bundles of fruit. Her sleeves were starched and high above her shoulder like butterfly wings. Her long black hair was pulled back into a stately bun. And propped on her nose, ready to slide off her face, sat a pair of rhinestone cat-eye glasses. Regular glasses.

"Why does *Lola* let him wear sun glasses?" They were clearly indoors.

"You know why, Tessa." Danilo turned a page and seeing the opportunity, Tessa crawled under the paper and into his lap.

"How did he lose his eye?" she asked as she pulled his face towards hers.

Resting her hands on the walls of his enormous face, she watched his expression. Her father was a handsome man. She knew it and all her friends said so too. "Did he look like you when he was young? I mean, except for the blind eye?" Tessa held onto Danilo firmly, waiting for him to tell her the story when David and Tony charged into the room.

"Tessa!" they shrieked. "Mom wants you to help her."

"Why can't you?" she asked them.

"We're boys!"

Danilo scooted her off his lap, and told her to help her mother in the kitchen. "We'll talk more later," he told her. "Or you know, what? You can ask him yourself, when he gets to the States."

She sighed, placing the photo back into her purse. "Okay, okay," she mumbled. "But when is he getting here?"

"Soon."

*

At dinner that night, she wondered about *Lolo*. She knew that during World War II he had been in the army. Maybe Japanese soldiers took his eye out in a fight. Maybe he had saved her father's barrio from destruction. Or maybe it was during a cock fight.

Her father liked to paint. All over their home, he painted oils of fantastic birds—red, orange, yellow raging birds. They were always suspended in mid-air, stunned and frozen. She remembered that her father used to sneak off to bet on these wild birds. He was always talking about getting caught by his dad. Maybe, she thought, *Lolo* found him in a cock ring when he was supposed to be in school. Maybe he grabbed her father's collar, just as a rooster flew right into his face. Maybe *Lolo* had saved him, and lived.

"Tessa," her mother said, "I asked you to pass the rice to Tony, okay, *hija*?"

"Sorry."

"I don't know about this girl, Daddy," her mother continued as she brushed her hand over her daughter's forehead. "Her head is always someplace else."

"I know what you mean, Nora," her father agreed. "She must get that from you, ha?"

"Sorry, Mom," she said again as she fingered the picture in her purse. She knew that photo so well, she knew where their faces were, could feel where the glasses interrupted the flow of his face. She was certain he had lost his eye heroically.

*

Her best friend, Carmen Hernandez, was always going to her Nana's and Poppa's house. She'd leave Tessa for entire weekends, which Tessa hated. She was always so bored when Carmen was gone. But then Carmen would bring back cookies and Mexican candy, piñatas and other new toys. Her Nana and Poppa were always giving Carmen presents. "It's their job," she told Tessa. "It's what grandparents do."

"I know," Tessa said. "You don't have to tell me."

"Too bad you don't have a nana and poppa."

"I have 'em. They just live in the Philippine Islands."

One Saturday, Carmen brought Tessa with her. The two girls spent most of Saturday morning sitting in a tree branch, spying on Nana. "She looks so young," Tessa whispered. She watched Nana pull a rack of cookies out of the oven, watched her springy head of black curls bob as she moved, watched as Nana puckered up her red lips and blew onto the hot tray.

"It's because she got married when she was thirteen," Carmen answered. She drew her legs close to her chest, hugging them. "That's how they do it in Mexico."

"Wow, I don't know when my *lola* married *Lolo*. But it must have been early too. She had seventeen babies, you know. Three of them died in the war." She pulled out the photo and showed it to Carmen. "Can you believe someone this pretty could have seventeen babies?"

"What war was that?" Carmen's pigtails were falling out of their red rubber bands.

"You know, World War II."

Carmen took the photo from her and squinted at it hard. "Too bad you've never met your nana and poppa, huh?"

She nodded her head and thought of her neighbor Charlie. Sometimes, Tessa sat at her bedroom window, watching Charlie with his grandkids. He liked building them things—forts, boats, wagons. Some afternoons he sat with them under his tree, telling stories about Poland, telling ridiculous jokes and riddles. It seemed no matter what Charlie said, they were always giggling and tickling and yelling. She thought they were so lucky.

*

Tessa and David were lying with their faces to the floor, waiting for Tony to come from the bedroom. Their dad was so mad. While he was in the garage and their mother was napping, they played. Now they were waiting to get it. David and Tessa lay with their bare bums to the sky. Tony was already crying and he hadn't even taken his pants down yet.

They had turned the kitchen table into an altar, pushed it up against the wall and smeared blue and red tempera paint on the windows to make them look like stained glass. They took the white bread from its narrow plastic bag and pressed it flat with bottles. Then they cut perfect little circles out of them with scissors. They made Holy Communion. David played the part of the priest, Tessa the lady in church and Tony acted like an altar boy. The crusts were brushed off their makeshift altar, onto the linoleum floor and the glass they had used to press the bread was also tossed to the floor. It had shattered like a giant church chime, splintered all over the floor and summoned their dad back into the house.

Now, they were waiting to get it. Danilo strutted around the family room, whacking his leather belt across his hand. He snapped and they shuddered. Tessa could hear Tony and she knew his face was red and blubbery. She could feel her bottom tense up every time Danilo cracked his belt.

"Tony," his father warned him, "pull your pants down. Now."

He cried and screamed, but eventually he pushed his pants to his ankles. Tessa peeked out of the cracks of her fingers, tasted the salt from them and started to giggle. Tony had pulled his pants down, alright, but he also had on ten pairs of underwear. She could see her father grinning, but still he scolded Tony.

"How many times have I told you kids not to be so wild?" WHACK! It was only the air. "Why do you mess the house like this? Can't your mommy get any sleep?" ZAM! He slapped the carpet next to Tessa. "Tony, you take all the pants off and join your brother and sister." He slashed the air with the belt, an old trick for their father, the disciplinarian. Tony screamed as though he'd been hit.

They were scared. And they cried. But he never spanked them. He hit the carpet around them, his hand, snapping the belt on belt, but he never hit them. He scared them and they promised to be good children forever more.

*

Tessa loved the weekends. On Sundays, after Mass, Tessa's parents, Danilo and Nora Villa always brought them to the county park. On this day, she felt the sun beating down on their metallic green station wagon and the hot air smothering them, invading the spaces between them. Tony and David leaned against the vinyl backs of the front seat, with their noses buried into their father's ear. They were singing the jingle to their favorite fast food place. "Such a hap hap happy place . . ." She thought they were annoying, as always.

"Come on, Tessa," David said, nudging her. "Sing and maybe Dad'll get the hint."

"That is so stupid," she told him. She socked him in the arm and he sang even louder.

"Settle down, kids," Danilo said. "When your *lolo* and *lola* come you're going to have to learn to be quiet."

"How?" Tony asked.

"What your dad means," Nora explained, "is that your grandparents aren't used to small children. You'll make them dizzy."

"That seems weird," Tessa jumped in. "I mean they had seventeen babies."

The station wagon entered the park, driving into a sea of Sunday people. Tessa could hear the twinkling of an ice cream truck some place on the grounds, the waves crashing on the man-made lake, and she wriggled in her seat. She couldn't wait to get out of the car. "So, are *Lolo* and *Lola* coming soon?" she asked. "Every week you say they're coming."

"That's because we've been saving to bring them here," Danilo said. "So my mom and dad can see this life too."

He pulled the wagon's nose into a diagonal of cars. Looking out, Tessa saw people walking without pattern, surrounding their car and screaming to people on the other side of the park.

They settled under an oak tree, not far from the lake and ate Kentucky Fried Chicken and cold rice on paper plates. After lunch, their father took a ball of string, some left over rice, the

Sunday paper, and a few tree branches and created a cartoon kite. He sculpted a "T" with the two sticks, held them together with a piece of string. He covered the frame with paper. The rice worked as glue, held the newspaper together like buttons on a coat, kept the corners of the kite square.

"This is how we made kites when I was a boy," he told them. Tessa watched her father's hands. They were long and dark. He worked quickly like a magic man.

"Your dad taught you," Tessa said. "Right? *Lolo*. Because they didn't have glue in your town and your dad showed you how to use rice for glue, right?"

"And he showed you how to make boats too," David said. Danilo took a couple grains of rice and smeared them into the newspaper. He folded another piece over that and pressed.

When Tessa and the boys grew tired of the kite, Danilo built them a boat out of the travel section, and hats from fashion. "Look, Ma," Tessa said, as she ran to her mother who sat under a tree, reading a book. She waved the paper toys in Nora's face, fanning a tiny breeze up. Tessa's bangs flew from her face, her hot, sweaty face. The sun had flushed her pink and her hair was damp. "You have *pawis*," Nora said as she brushed the perspiration from her daughter's face. "I know," Tessa told her. Meanwhile, Danilo folded the rest of the paper into birds and animals that lived in a jungle on their picnic table. With magical words, he made the animals live and suddenly Tessa and the boys were the elephant, they were the tiger, the monkey. They acted like animals flying kites. They were the kites flying like birds, zipping across the light blue space, the sky.

*

On Friday night, the Villas threw a dinner party. They invited Carmen's parents, Uncle Tommy, Auntie Baby and Dr. Santos and his mother. She had just arrived from the Philippines and Tessa could not stop following her about. She was pretending Mrs. Santos was her grandmother's best friend, or better yet, that she was her grandmother. Mrs. Santos wore her hair exactly as her *lola* did in the photo. All night, the old woman sat quietly in a corner, away from the action, speaking occasionally, nodding to those who could not speak her language. Smiling always.

Tessa approached her and looked into her eyes. She took Mrs. Santos' hand and brought it to her forehead. When Tessa looked up, she saw the old woman giggling. Mrs. Santos pulled Tessa's face towards hers and pressed her pink powdered cheek next to Tessa's. Her face was full of soft wrinkles that wrapped itself in rings the way trees make rings in the passing of time.

"She knows how to make *mano?*" Dr. Santos shouted. "That's amazing that a child from this country knows how to make *mano*." He reached down to pat Tessa's head. "Good for you, *hija*. It's good to see kids still respecting their elders."

"She's practicing for her own *lola*," Danilo said. "Aren't you, sweetheart?" Tessa beamed, stood tall. Yes, she thought, I am.

*

Carmen, Tony, David and Tessa sat in the kitchen, eating at the children's table. They were low to the ground, in a world of their own as the grown-ups whizzed about them, talking at once, laughing at everything, hearing absolutely nothing.

From where she sat, she could see slips hanging from skirts, high heels piercing the toes of leather shoes and pant legs being hoisted as they took their places in the dining room next door. She watched Mrs. Santos shuffle her old feet under the table. Her legs were brown and bare. She wore straw slippers, embroidered with bright flowers like the hemp purse Tessa wore around her neck.

"Leave me alone," Carmen said as she pulled her hand away from David. "Just eat your own food."

"Shhht," Tessa warned them. Standing from the table, she motioned Carmen to follow. They crouched their bodies so low, they felt invisible, tiny like mice shooting from behind the china cabinet.

They listened to the low garble of conversation filter out of the adult mouths, teetering in the air like bubbles in a cartoon strip.

"They talk weird," Carmen whispered.

"That's their accent, dummy," Tessa whispered back. "Your nana has one too, you know."

"Not like that she doesn't."

The grown-ups sit at a rectangular table, Tessa's parents on either end, their guests between them, evenly spaced, with elbows at their sides. There was no shoving. Danilo's voice loomed out above the others.

"When I was a boy," he said gesturing to himself, "I wanted to see MacArthur talk at Rizal Square for myself. So I told my mother I was going to school and instead, I hitchhiked my way there."

"How old were you, Danilo?" Carmen's mother asked.

"Old enough to know better," said Auntie Baby.

"A black American soldier picked me up in his jeep. I gave him a few cigarettes and he drove me to Rizal."

"This is the kind of talk I want to keep away from the children," Nora said.

Tessa turned to Carmen and whispered, "I love that story. He never gets in trouble either. . . ."

"Better we tell the kids than my folks tell them—they'd make it sound so much worse."

Dr. Santos leaned back in his chair, lit up a cigarette. "Are they coming soon?" he asked. The doctor was round. He had a round head, round eyes and a mouth like a golf hole. He had stocky little fingers with a belly to match. Tessa noted that all his roundness was puffed with her mother's cooking.

"They should be left alone," said Uncle Tommy. "They should live out their days back home, where they're comfortable. Where they are respected." Uncle Tommy rocked forward as he spoke. Tessa thought of the nights the three Villa siblings sat at their kitchen table arguing. Uncle Tommy would turn red in the face, would sway like a tree in a storm with every point he made. He didn't want his mom and dad to come here. Auntie Baby spoke as loudly as Uncle Tommy. Only she was trying to mediate because, as always, Danilo was the loudest. His voice would cover all the noise, the shouting and he would punctuate his sentences by pounding his heavy fists on the table. Auntie Baby always ended up crying.

"Life's hard back there," Danilo answered. "You know we've finally gotten ourselves settled. My work, the house, and Nora and the kids."

"I still think it's unfair," said Uncle Tommy. "What makes you think Mommy and Daddy want to come here?"

"Are the papers ready?" Dr. Santos wanted to know. He blew smoke out of his mouth, puffed like a train so that the rings linked together and floated to the ceiling.

"I've been told they should be in order by the end of the month," Danilo answered.

Finally, a date, a commitment, Tessa thought. Something to look forward to. Her father would never give her a date, but his friends? In a month she would have a *lola* and *lolo* like Carmen's.

*

That Monday, around six o'clock, the phone rang. Sitting in the dark, Tessa watched *I Love Lucy* on channel thirteen. She could hear her mother in the kitchen. She could hear the lights sizzling with grease, vegetables spinning and slipping across the surface of her hot frying pan, water gurgling to a boil and a fan swirling relentlessly above the stove. She patted her tummy and thought of how hungry she was. David and Tony raced up and down stairs, reenacting that day's *Batman* episode. Every time they ran past her, she screamed at them and rolled her eyes. What babies. The phone kept ringing, but no one answered it. They were all busy.

The Villa house seemed to vibrate with sound no one heard. Maybe because noise was a part of their house, like air and electricity and dust, noise was always there. They ignored it. Except

Tessa, she heard everything. Even though Ricky Ricardo stood before her in a light box, crooning "Babaloo," she still heard the motor of the garage door as it rose. She felt her father's footsteps as he entered their home. She even heard the phone ringing, but she didn't answer it. She heard Danilo squeak a kiss onto Nora's lips. Then he answered the phone.

She heard everything, except her father's conversation. But then, she was more concerned with how funny Lucy was tonight. Still, she felt weird. For once, her father's voice wasn't booming into the phone. Usually it carried above all the noise and that voice was Tessa's comfort. It was how she knew she was home.

She turned from the TV and saw his silhouette. His long body bent, his chin falling softly onto his chest. He spoke in an almost whisper. She strained her eyes to see the expression of his face, but it was too dark. She couldn't tell what he was speaking of, but she knew it was something awful.

He placed the phone back into its cradle and walked into the family room. Without taking off his overcoat, he sat down on the brown leather recliner and slowly folded his legs under himself.

Tessa had never seen her father cry. Her mother came into the room and quietly he told her that his father had died. In his sleep, he died. She leaned over him, held him the way she holds Tony or David when they've fallen. She rocked his body as the sobbing grew louder.

David and Tony ran into the room, still garbed in blue and red capes. Silently they stood next to Tessa and watched. The house was quiet except for her father's cries. The children looked at each other and then their parents. The only thing they knew was to be quiet.

Later that night, Nora tried to feed them, but they couldn't eat. The sound of their father crying bothered Tessa, made her feel sick. He was still sitting in the family room, rocking. Dinner grew cold and no one could eat.

All night long, their father curled up in his chair and wept. Wrapping his arms around himself he rolled in the arms of that

recliner. Cooing, he chanted, "My daddy, my daddy, my daddy."
He didn't know it, but Tony, David and Tessa kept him company.
From the top of the stairs they watched over him. Tessa thought
he looked different, like someone else, a stranger maybe. He
rocked from side to side and rubbed his eyes. His face was red like
Tony's when he was hurt. Sometimes he whimpered soft and low,
other times that night he howled and pounded his fists into the
arms of the chair, uttering words Tessa didn't understand. She
thought he might be going mad.

*

Tessa was nervous, her stomach was tight and as her parents
moved about, she kept looking over her shoulder at her dad. She
was worried. Danilo had gone to the Philippines and when he
came back he brought with him all kinds of Filipino cookies and
candy—little pastries in shapes of boats with icing doodles, can-
died tamarind fruit rolled in sugar and even a few bamboo toys
and tops. These things Tessa loved. He also brought with him a
movie of *Lolo*'s funeral. She had never been to a funeral and was
not sure what to expect.

Tessa and the boys sat in a row on their shag carpet. Above the
doorway, between the kitchen and family room, Nora had hung a
bed sheet, creating a makeshift screen.

"Ready?" Danilo asked as he finished threading the projector.

Their mother leaned over and flipped off the lights. Tessa
grabbed Tony's hand, squeezed it. Nobody spoke, only the click-
click-purr of the projector could be heard. For a moment, they
were suspended in black, not knowing what to expect. Not knowing if they should be curious or scared or sad.

She glanced at her father again and thought she saw him crying, then she turned to the wall and saw. On the sheet before her,
they carried *Lolo* above their heads, proceeding slowly along the
unpaved streets of Danilo's barrio. Gliding before his casket was a
statue of the Blessed Virgin. Her skin, white and veiled in porcelain, adorned with bright flowers, looked soft against the grain of

the super-eight camera. The mourners were lined up ten across and one mile long. People of his town. Heads bowed up and down the lines, while women pulled black lace over their heads, rubbing their beads and whispering something Tessa couldn't hear. Amid the crowd were pockets of umbrellas, shutting out the sun, the light. The camera skipped back and forth and back, in search of her father, her *lola*, the rest of her aunts and uncles. It looked for cousins Tessa had never met. But everyone was in black, or hidden behind their darkest pair of sun glasses and Tessa could not find one familiar face. Every now and then, a jagged movement towards the camera suggested a wave, a recognition of some kind. And each time the camera nodded back politely.

Tessa closed her eyes quickly. She rubbed. And when she opened them wide and round, she focused on the coffin, floating above the people. Gently they placed it down. They opened it. A plate of glass upon the casket separated him from them. Tessa could see his face, slightly ashen and green, somewhat older than her photo, but as defined and striking as she had pictured *Lolo*. He lay in a bed of flowers, the same kind that dressed Mary's statue. The sun glasses were gone. His eyes were closed. And it didn't matter that one eye was blind, but Tessa still wanted to know, which one?

For a moment, the camera was still and the crowd appeared to be hushed. Tessa was still searching for her grandmother, she knew *Lola* must be near. After the silence, there was a fluttering motion at the head of the casket. Tessa leaned forward, trying somehow to slip into the scene, crawl onto the sheet on the wall. She found her *lola* and she wanted to go to her. Her arms, draped in a long black veil, shooed them away, fluttering about them like the ruffled feathers of an angry, wild bird. *Lola's* fists, clenched at the edges of her black veil, flying about like ruffled feathers of an angry, wild bird. She used her body to cover the glass plate, to keep from the good-bye. Tessa thought she heard her sobbing. *Lola* wouldn't let anyone put their arms on her. She let no one get between her and her husband.

Now in their family room, Tessa reached for her father and placed her arms around his neck. She could no longer keep from crying. "So many people," she whispered to him. And from her hemp purse, she pulled out a picture, showed him. She let him touch it, rub it to life like a genie lamp, like a wish waiting to come true. She offered her photo to him so he could make it come to life, bringing *Lolo* to them, the way she always did.

CONTRAVIDA

Lisa's father picks her up at O'Hare airport and they drive along the outskirts of the city, weaving past forest preserves in Evanston, Skokie, and Niles. From the car's dusty window, she watches barren trees sculpt the night, black on black figures that make her think of widows and witches with lean and bony limbs. Make her think of curses and spells, like the ones her *Tita* Lina was so good at casting. Make her think of death. She squints at the edge of the city, watches lights blink white and red. She imagines they are warning her, telling her not to come.

"They're all waiting," says her father. He pushes the lighter into the socket, slips a cigarette between his lips and breathes. That's what I'm afraid of, she thinks.

Rolling the window down, she says, "I get kind of queasy."

He nods, turns the lighter off. "Your mom used to get nauseous over everything. We had to give up garlic and fish and all kinds of cheese. Even *she* gave up smoking."

"How's Mom doing?" she asks. Her mother had gone into the hospital last week for what the doctors called a look-see. When she woke hours later, they told her they had found cancer cells lined up in the walls of her fallopian tubes.

"She's still weak, but I think she's happy everyone's here," her father says.

Lisa glances at him. She notices that his hair has peppered itself silver gray. Suddenly she sees him sitting alone like this in the car or at the kitchen table. "Well, Mom'll be back on her feet real soon," she says. She rolls down her window further and breathes in the night air.

"How about you, *hija?*" He reaches his hand over and pats her tummy. "How are you two doing?"

"Fine, fine, Dad. We're both scared to death, that's what we are." She wishes the rest of the family hadn't come home too. She had spent the last few years avoiding them and their gossip. If it wasn't for her mom, she would have stayed away. At least Lisa's parents understood her situation, or rather have come to understand it. The others would not. "Brother, I can just imagine *Tita* Lina's face. Not only was I a disrespectful niece, but now I've disgraced the Santiago name. It'll go something like that, don't you think, Dad?"

After living on her own for years, away from her parents, her aunts and uncles and all the rules and traditions, Lisa stopped asking for advice. She moved first to Chicago, into the film ghetto in Wicker Park, picking up paper plates and seltzer bottles on sets, cleaning up after directors and producers, making breakfasts and lunches and snacks for the crew. A hundred bucks a day. She learned the business by making bagel runs, hiding donuts for temperamental actresses and crabby set stylists. She worked her way up the ladder from craft service to production assistant all the way to assistant camera. In New York, Lisa worked as the director of photography on several low budget documentaries, for free. Just to get started.

*

They exit the expressway and the car drives along harshly lit strip malls and gas stations, fast food joints and convenience stores. "What's all this?" she asks her father.

"Development, *hija,*" he tells her. "Change. Everything is changing."

I'll say, she thinks. There was a time when she looked forward to going home. Tonight she feels both excited and terrified. She rubs her hands around the swelling of her abdomen. The baby's turning over, spinning inside of her, trying to get comfortable. You can try, she thinks, but this weekend's a tough one. I doubt you'll sleep, my baby.

She was seeing Danny in an on-again-off-again way. He was a nice man who often made her batty with his meticulous manner. He never saw the big picture and she often told him to "Get over your bad self" when she really wanted to slap him. And when her litmus paper turned pink, she decided to keep the baby, and break her on-again-off-again habit with Danny. "How 'bout we stop sleeping together," she told him, "and you can help me with the baby?" It took him a while before he could decide, but ultimately, he had to say yes.

She imagines *Tita* Lina has cornered each and every family member and told them about the fight. She'll serve that info like an appetizer, then she'll offer them the big course, the whopper. Lisa, the out-of-wedlock-monster-mother. She can see the old woman's eyes light up, her arms gesturing like fire to the sky. She knows how to draw her listeners in, seducing them. Lisa pictures her old aunt's fist pounding at her chest, her lower lip trembling. "I loved her the most," *Tita* Lina would say. "That girl was my favorite." She'd cast a spell on all of them.

*

The car quietly slips past houses. Lisa can see into some of the living rooms. There are children lying on carpets, heads lifted towards the television. A woman is sitting in an easy chair with a book. There is a man coming out of his house with a poodle on a leash. Home. The neighborhood has not changed much, she thinks. Perhaps it has aged—the trees look bigger, their trunks thicker, branches heavier. The paint on houses are more worn and paler than when she was home last. Where she lives in New York, there are no single dwellings. People live on top of one another, are shimmied into shoe-box apartments, shoulder to shoulder. There, the streets are lined with lamp posts, and at midnight, you can see as bright as day. Looking onto the street and lawns here in the 'burbs, darkness settles in bushes and flower beds, about circular driveways and manicured alleyways. This kind of low visibility scares Lisa. Makes her think of unsafe things.

"So," she says, sighing. "Has *Tita* Lina turned the whole family against me?"

"Don't talk like that, *hija*. You don't have to be the *contravida*, you're old enough to understand."

"Right, I should keep quiet."

When she visited *Tita* Lina six years ago, she was in between film jobs and boyfriends. In her kitchen, Lina had dragged Lisa's hands across the table and held them to her chest. *Tita* Lina told Lisa of all the others' misdeeds, how they had gotten too busy and too proud to remember their old aunt. How she sat up nights counting the times they had broken her heart. How she had cried. "Except for you, darling," she had told Lisa. "You are my *vida*, my star."

In the afternoon light, her aunt's face grew heavy with lines, her voice went hoarse, the corners of her mouth drooped, lay parallel to her rumpled eyebrows. Lisa couldn't help feeling trapped. A week of this, she thought.

"Do you get lonely?" Lisa had asked.

"Of course I do," Lina answered. "Wait till death takes the one you love." Tears slipped from the corners of her eyes. She wiped them away with a stroke of her hand then pounded her chest with her fist. Thump, thump, thump. Dramatic as always. "My husband is dead and everyone has forgotten me. What do you expect?"

*

When she first enters the house, she hears the voices, the music and the weight of children as they chase each other up and down the steps of the house. The aroma of stir fry, chicken and pork marinated in garlic, onions, *toyo,* and lemon waft from the kitchen to the door. She smells jasmine rice. Everything is as she had imagined, everything is in chaos. Her father bellows into the hallway, calling out, "Hello, hello! Look what I brought home! Look who's here."

"Where's Mom?" Lisa asks her sister Dessa. She looks about at all the faces, searching. "Where is she?" she asks again. Lisa thinks that suddenly there's silence. As if God or someone looking down on them has pushed the mute button on the remote. What are you looking at, she wants to say. At my stomach? But no one mentions the baby. Several of the relatives gather round her and kiss her, but she notices how uncomfortable they are, shifting on their feet, speaking to her forehead, her ear, the center of her flat nose, but never speaking to her. Never looking right at her.

"What a trip," Lisa tells them. "My feet are swollen and I feel as big as that Marshmallow Stay Puff Man from *Ghostbusters.*"

They laugh nervously—her *tita*s and uncles. They tell her, yes, yes, travel is exhausting, but she's young. Maybe she's not eating right?

"Well, no," she answers smiling. "I've *got* to eat right. I think it's just being pregnant. You know?" They smile and slip away. They tell her that her mommy is up in the bedroom resting. "Go wake her," they say. "She's been waiting."

Dessa walks Lisa through the house, dragging her by the hand and talking at once. "God are you pregnant," she tells her. Lisa brushes past children in the halls, kisses another aunt or two on the way.

She finds her mother lying in a nest of pillows and cushions, quilts and comforters. Her face is pale, a weak yellow. Her mouth has slipped open a little, and tiny spasms of breath escape her as she sleeps.

"Mommy?" she says. As Lisa nears the bed, she places a hand on the mattress, and balancing her weight carefully she lays her body down. "Mom, it's Lisa. Wake up." When she opens her eyes, she smiles.

"Why are you crying you stupid girl? I'm fine," she says, rubbing Lisa's belly. "Who's this?"

Lisa squeezes her mother's hand. An image of her mom with Dessa bundled up like a doll in her arms zips through her mind. "Must be those damn hormones," Lisa utters. She sits up and looks out the window. "Where is *Tita* Lina?"

"She's taking a nap," Dessa tells them.

Her mother runs her hands over Lisa's face, washing the tears from them. "Now, you don't upset your Auntie, huh? You're an adult now, be patient with her."

"Yeah, yeah, yeah. I know." Lisa looks up at her and laughing she says, "So, she hasn't banned me from the house, then?"

*

In the hall, two small children run past her. They are barefoot and round like cub bears. Lisa bends down and scoops a child into her arms. "So, what'd the doctor say," she asks Dessa.

"She says they got it all—they think."

"Oh yeah?" Lisa kisses the child's belly. "Who are you?" she asks. "Who are you?" The little boy squirms in her arms, pushing at her chest to be let go. He begins crying. Slipping from her grasp, he jumps to the floor.

"Has *Tita* Lina brainwashed that one?" she asks, feeling rejected.

"Stop being so paranoid," Dessa says. "Mike's only two and he's never met you. Why shouldn't he be scared?"

Around the corner, she sees her older cousin wrestling with a toddler. "*Ate* Gina," she calls, walking toward her. Gina smiles as she turns the baby loose. Her hair is bobbed and swings into her eyes. Running her hand over her face she sighs and pecks Lisa on the cheek.

"Hey stranger," she says. Behind them, her baby pulls books out of the shelf and tosses them onto the floor. "Oops, gotta go," she tells her. Lisa watches her run for the baby, cuddle her in her arms. "Are you wet? Is this a soggy diaper?" she asks, sticking a finger into the baby's diaper.

They don't look at her belly which has grown big and fat these last seven months. Am I paranoid, she wonders. Or maybe I'm not pregnant, I only think I am. But when the baby starts her daily exercise, flipping and swimming about the pool inside of her, she knows it isn't her, it's them.

*

As they set the tables for dinner, Lisa asks her sister about *Tita* Lina. "How's she doing?" They're walking around the tables, one trailing after the other. Lisa places a plate down, Dessa sets a napkin next to it. Cousins run in between them, weave about their legs.

"Feisty," Dessa tells her. "Still trying to get Mike and me married."

So, Lisa thinks, she's still pushing people around. At her cousin Gina's wedding, *Tita* Lina dragged Lisa up to her cousin who was costumed in white satin and lace, veiled and beautiful, and said, "This should be you, darling. You could be this." Gina had thrown Lisa a sympathetic look, hugged her and said, "Pay no attention to her." In a corner of the dimly lit ballroom, Lina then interrogated Lisa's date, a shy man who seemed to glow red all evening long. They had only been dating for two months and Lisa had really liked him. She thought her aunt had something to do with their breakup the following week. Lisa places a plate down hard, nearly breaking it. "What a pain. Doesn't she understand that women can be women without getting married?"

"Actually," Dessa says, "we're talking about it. Me and Mike. Getting married I mean."

The voices in the house rise, compete against the stereo blasting top forty hits and one of the boys drumming on their brothers' old snare. They toss each other looks.

"So, Mom's supposed to get well with all these people in her house? What are they, crazy?" She pulls silverware from the drawer.

She listens, hoping to hear individual voices and phrases, hoping to recognize a conversation, but it's all noise to her—the music is nothing more than the continual thump of a bass, the children's screams clash with the banging of the snare drum. When she looks up, Lulu, Gina's seven year old, is watching her. The child is wearing floral leggings and an oversized T-shirt, a baseball cap sits crooked on her head. Lisa smiles at her and starts counting forks, spoons and knives.

"Are you going to have a baby?" she asks. Lisa nods her head. Lulu points at her stomach. "Pretty fat."

"Yep," Lisa tells her. She loses count, starts over.

"Where's your husband?"

Lisa pulls the forks out of the drawer rapidly, drops several of them at once. Silverware collides in a shattering of metals.

*

The night of the fight, Lisa and *Tita* Lina dined on the terrace, bathing in an orange-red sunset, surrounded by the walls of Lina's lilac bushes. The flowers, sweet and suffocating, perfumed the garden. *Tita* Lina kissed the tea cup as she drank and left red lip-stick stains on the gold rim of the china. "*Ay*, Lisa," she said as she fingered Lisa's hair. "I was like you too—I liked to record things. Make pictures."

"I shoot film, *Tita*," Lisa told her, "documentaries."

Tita Lina pulled Lisa's hair back and began to braid the strands. "You are so photogenic. You should be in movies, *hija*. You could be the star, the *vida*."

Tita Lina went on to list several Filipina stars, glamorous women who always played romantic love scenes, who always won her man and married him. "Did you know, *hija*, that *vida* is Spanish for life. You could be the life in Filipino Hollywood."

Lisa picked up her glass and drank the wine quickly. She felt the red drink burn the back of her throat, flush her forehead and cheeks.

"It's a shame," Lina said. She cupped her niece's face close to her own and sang, "So beautiful, huh? Like a *modelo*. Why did you stop?"

"Because I wanted to direct films, *Tita*, not be in them."

"At least if you want a career, be on TV and maybe a good man will see you," she said. "I know what I mean, *hija*. Your Uncle Harry was my life—now I have nothing. Death came just like that." She snapped her fingers. "Sometimes I regret not being blessed with our own children—don't end up like this, *anak*."

Lisa looked into the sun, at the thin streaks of clouds that had been colored pink and orange. The old woman was goading her, and she was trying to be respectful. She felt the heat spreading fast across her cheeks. Downing the rest of her wine and placing the glass firmly back on the table, she worked to keep her voice from tripping, stammering, falling out of place.

"I'm not your *anak*," Lisa whispered. "I have a mother."

Lisa remembers how her ears were clouded by silence, how her anger pushed her to fight back. In that instant there was a flash, like a picture had been taken or the moment stuck like a needle on a record. She stood frozen, waiting for Lina to retaliate. But, the old aunt turned away from her, the favorite niece, the god-child, and went into the house.

*

Lisa closes her eyes, sees a full and fleshy face, eyebrows arched high and penciled in. Her auntie's wide mouth smiles at her in lush red colors as her dimples crease long and deep. A scent of lilacs floats by. A strong hand kneads the knots across Lisa's shoulders, says, "Is this how you treat your elders, *hija*?" Shivers—tiny, piercing shivers—scuttle down her back, ice chills her skin. "How long have you been here? Why haven't you come to greet me?"

She looks up over her shoulder, and Lina stands over her smiling, her silver tooth twinkling. "Hello Auntie," Lisa stutters. "They told me you were napping."

"Hours ago," she answers. Lina pulls her up and runs her hands along Lisa's arms, reads her face with her palms. "You are not eating," she tells her as she walks into the kitchen. "Too skinny."

Lisa looks down at her stomach. "How can you say I'm too

skinny? Look at me." She gestures down her body. "I'm at least twenty pounds heavier than the last time you saw me."

"You look weak and sickly. Girl your age should take better care. Especially now," she says. "Your mama needs you to take care of her." She walks away from Lisa. Her perfume trails after her, an invisible cloud. Lisa watches her pinching the other nephews and nieces, kissing their faces as she goes.

Lisa feels her face redden. The tips of her fingers tingle, sending tiny charges up her arms, her legs and feet. What is the matter with that old woman, she wonders. She opens her mouth, about to speak, when Gina brushes past her, tugs at her sleeve and shakes her head. "Shh," she whispers. "Not now."

*

At dinner, Lisa sits in her old seat, across from her sister and kitty-corner from her father. The table has been expanded to fit twelve adults with a child or two between them. Usually her mother sits at the other end of the table, but tonight *Tita* Lina holds court there. The matriarch speaks family histories, teasing everyone there including Lisa. "I love all my nieces and nephews," she says raising a glass of wine. "Especially my successful ones like you Gina and Dessa. Lulu is growing up to be a fine young woman too. A Santiago." *Tita* Lina blows a kiss. Then she pulls out a long and slender cigarette and lights up. Leaning over, she whispers in a loud and still confidential way, "You know I ran into Carlotta Ruben the other day. She was a girl from my village who was always running around with men. She was crazy. The first time she was with child and no husband, the family disowned her. By the second time, she was dead to them. Yet by her fourth child, her mother took pity on her and sent her to Carlotta's auntie in the States. Her auntie took care of her for years. Gave her a home. Some decency. Now she's an old woman like me, with dozens of grandchildren. Those poor Rubens . . ." She shakes her head and clicks her tongue and everyone nods their head in agreement.

"I suppose a lot of that has to do with the family," *Tito* Ernesto says.

"It has to do with those Americans!" Lina said. "See what happened to those wicked girls in Olongapo. Can you imagine?"

Lisa sits quietly at her place, not looking up. She can feel her cousins throwing glances at her, wondering what she will do. Nothing, she thinks, I'll do nothing. Looking around the table, she tosses Dessa a look. But Dessa only shakes her head, whispers, "Don't." The table is full, she thinks, crowded and noisy. When she glances up to where her mother would be, Lina sneers. Just like an old witch, she thinks. Lisa feels warm, the food makes her hot and the steam from the rice dampens her brow.

"Although," Lisa's father says, "times have changed. Young women don't always have babies by accident. Sometimes they want them."

"But without a father?" Lina blurts out. "Ridiculous. Immoral." Lina blows rings of smoke out of her red painted lips, waves her freckled hand in the air and wafts the smoke to the center of the room.

The air thickens with smoke as Lina continues to tell stories, slips like poison into Lisa's lungs and makes her woozy. "*Tita*," she says as she waves her hands in front of her. "Do you mind? It's making me sick."

"Ha?" *Tita* Lina shouts. "You want one too? I forgot you're a smoker."

"No," Tony says. "I think she wants you to put that out, *Ate* Lina. It's bad for the baby."

"She's a grown woman, if she doesn't like it she can leave the table." *Tita* Lina stares at her. Slips the cigarette into her mouth, inhales deeply then blows. She smiles at Lisa.

"I'm going to check on Mom," Lisa says. She shoves her chair out, knocking her water glass into her plate, soaking the table, the serving plates and other dishes. She leaves the room, the chaos at the table. Nothing new for the Santiagos. You clean it up, she thinks.

*

She slips under the covers of her mother's bed, nestling next to her. She watches her mother sleep. Delicate lines etched her face like the cracks in porcelain china. Gray tempers her dark hair. Lisa watches the fall and rise of her mother's breath and imagines how she once lived inside her belly too. When she wakes, Lisa asks her, "Are you okay, Ma? Do you maybe want something to eat?"

"What's wrong, *hija?*"

"Nothing. Do you feel different, Ma? I mean since the operation? Do you feel, you know?"

"Not really. I thought I would—but I'm still the same woman. Why, do I look different to you?"

She shakes her head no, then tells her mother she does feel different. "I'm always crying and I let people get to me."

"You mean your *Tita* Lina?"

Dessa walks into the room, placing herself at the end of the bed.

"You shouldn't let her get to you," Dessa whispers.

"I don't understand why no one in this family tells her she's crazy. She is," Lisa says.

Her mother pulls herself up from the bed, trying to sit, but she only slides back down into a mountain of pillows. Lisa shudders. They say they got it all, but who makes guarantees anymore? Not doctors. She runs her hands along her arms, brushing the shivers away. "Did you want to eat?" Lisa asks. Her mother shakes her head. "Can I get you something, Mommy?"

"You should have heard *Tita* Lina at dinner," Dessa says.

Lisa nods and tells her mother, "You should have been there to shut her up. You're the only one who can, you know."

"You girls should learn how to deal with her, you're adults now. And besides, I won't always be around."

"Don't talk like that, Mom," Lisa snaps.

"It's true," her mother says. She closes her eyes, the muscles in her face relaxing and the lines there fold neatly under her chin, her eyes, the corners of her mouth. "You know your Auntie Lina has always been a *contravida*," she tells them, still with her eyes shut. Lisa looks over at her sister, who looks away towards the floor. This really sucks, she thinks.

"Anyway, Dessa, I was just asking Mom if she still has a sex drive—do you? You still want to do it with Dad?"

"Lisa!" Dessa says, laughing as she pushes her tears away with the back of her hand. "I don't want to know that."

The baby moves. She juts a foot or a hand out the side of Lisa's belly. The women place their hands there. Follow the movement. Bless it. Their palms circle the child, slip over each other. They lie there, giggling and talking and soon they are crying, grateful that everything has turned out okay. "We'll all be fine," their mother said. "You're good girls. Never second guess your choices."

*

Tita Lina fixes her makeup, touching up her red lipstick, brushing on beige powder and penciling in her faded brow. She stoops under the spotlight of the vanity mirror. Like an aging actress she examines her face, pulling at her cheeks and eyebrows, puckering her lips, and frowning. For a moment, Lisa stands in the doorway, watching Lina dip a brush into the pot of red. Her hands are frail and they tremble as one hand holds her mouth open and the other traces her lip line. *Tita* Lina slips and red smears at the corner of her mouth. Flustered, she grabs a tissue to wipe the lipstick. It's then that Lisa sees despite her auntie's performance, she's grown old, old and shaky.

"*Tita*," Lisa says.

Still facing the mirror, Lina's eyes widen when she sees Lisa's reflection in the mirror. "Come in, *hija*," she says. "Come in."

"*Tita*," she says. "I need to talk to you."

"You want me to be the star in your next movie, Miss Director?" she asks her. Lina brushes her eyebrows up with the tip of her finger. "I will consider it. I have always been a *vida* anyhow. I was very beautiful too, you know."

Lisa begins to speak and then she sees *Tita* Lina's pale face, her soft skin rippled and dry like an aging potato. *Tita* Lina stumbles, slipping gently, and reaches out her hand. Lisa helps steady her, holds her up with the weight of her own swollen arms.

"*Tita*," she says, as she runs her palm over her stomach. "I need you to understand."

"What?" Lina says. Crossing her arms, she leans towards Lisa. "Understand what, *hija*? I forgive you."

"But I don't think you have." Lisa looks down at her stomach, sees how it's grown huge, distorted its way out of her body. She thinks of sore thumbs and that cliche, what did it mean, to stick out like a sore thumb? "For one thing, I said what I did because you wouldn't let up. You pushed me."

"Silly child, I was only looking out for you and if you don't want me to love you and look out for you, I won't say anything at all. I was being your auntie, and you slapped me. *You pushed me.*"

Tita Lina turns back to the mirror, combing her eyebrows with a miniature brush. She takes a comb and teases her hair up into little spikes. "If I can't give you my advice, then I don't know how else to be your auntie. So maybe I'm not your auntie."

"But *Tita*," Lisa says. "Don't you want to know what I'm going through right now?"

"How your mommy and daddy can let you in this house in your condition, I don't know. But I don't say anything, because I'm no longer allowed to. As you said many years ago, what you do is not my business. How you will survive, feed that child, educate her, how you will face God without a man to help you—that is your life, not mine."

Lisa feels as though she's about to shout, to lose her temper all over again. And just as she's ready to spit anger, the baby kicks her. "She's always moving," Lisa whispers. "I can tell she's a feisty one."

Tita Lina shakes her head and frowns. "A *contravida*, no doubt. With a stubborn mind of her own," she says. Lisa leans over and takes her aunt's hand again.

"Come on, *Tita*," she says. "It's okay."

"This is unnatural," *Tita* Lina says. "In my day, we never touched the mother's stomach."

"That's hard to believe, Auntie," she says. She smiles at Lina, nods her head, whispers, "Come on, Auntie, try."

Lina lets Lisa take her, lead her, circle her belly. Lisa closes her eyes, her aunt's hand is tentative, soft, like spring rain, a drizzle. She pushes her aunt's palm flat, where the baby's foot is kicking. There, she thinks, there she is. Lina's hand relaxes, claiming a space on the equator of Lisa's stomach.

"*Naku*! She's strong." Leaning her head down, she places her cheek to Lisa's belly and listens.

*

In a year, Lisa will carry a cake out from the kitchen, and *Tita* Lina will be more concerned with capturing the moment than the baby, the cake, the presents or even the song. She'll shoo the men from their cameras. "*Shhhht* . . . I'll take it," she'll say. Lisa will watch her, anticipating her action, knowing what will happen next, the way she knows what happens next in those old movies, those reruns from black and white days. When were our days black and white? she'll wonder. Pinching and swatting them, Lina will herd the men around that table and point a camcorder up to the voices as they sing to Lisa's baby on her first birthday. Lisa will think about her own mother, wishing she could have been the one to carry the cake out, thinking, somehow, she is still with them. And the family will not look towards the child, they will smile into the lens. *Tita* Lina will shoot that video and cry out, "Oh look at my little *vida*! Such a star, such a sweetheart!" And the baby will burst out laughing.

MISS TEENAGE SAMPAGUITA

In the Philippines, my brother Frank and I grew up in a house where our father knew everything. *Tatay* would come home from work and the twelve of us would be sitting in chairs or lying on the floor; playing a game or reading to each other. He would start by describing the condition of the house—the way the lights were on in every room; the sandals and slippers thrown in a heap at the door; T-shirts, crumpled like rags in the bottom cushions of the love-seat my mother had worked so hard to upholster. Even though many of us were lying with our feet up in the air, a leg swinging up and down, reading, he complained that the books piled high to the ceiling and stacked like bricks along the base of the floor cluttered the room and obstructed his path. Why was no one reading them? Why was no one moving? We were all as lazy as flies. Then he would describe each and every one of us in detail and focus on the enormous flaws in our character. How he was working hard for us and the least we could do is work on our personal flaws and make our *tatay* happy. One by one we silently left the room. Each one sneaking out when his back was turned, or when he had gone into another room to turn another switch off. He said we were acting like hotel guests, coming and going as we pleased, never helping our poor mother, our overworked and under-loved mother. We were as lazy as hired hands on a Sunday. I can still hear the way his voice entered the house, took hold of all of us, invaded our peace like the Japanese had when they invaded our village years before. It was as though he were the enemy.

And now, on my own, away from my husband and kids, I sit at my brother's table where he leans back on the legs of his wooden chair, a toothpick in his mouth, ordering the youngest of his three children about.

"Millicent, you get your auntie something to drink," he says. "Baby, what do you want to drink? Millicent will get it for you."

"It's okay, it's okay," I tell him. "I'm fine." I want to tell him to shut up. I want to say, relax. What's going on? What is he doing? When Millicent stretches across the table, her long brown torso reaches from one end to the other. Her eyes, wide and dark as a chestnut horse, gaze over our heads. She moves silently around the table like a spirit, haunting us as she fills a glass full of ice water or tucks a paper napkin underneath a plate. She doesn't smile.

"Millicent," my brother yells to me, "is a good girl. She's smart. Aren't you smart, *hija*?" He tugs at her arm as she moves past him and places a fork at the side of his porcelain plate. "I want Millicent to go to John Hopkins for medicine."

Millie keeps moving, laying down silverware—fork, spoon, knife, fork, spoon, knife. He continues: "Going to be a doctor like her daddy, right, Millicent?"

Only now does she open her mouth, and when she does a glittering row of silver shines when she speaks. "But what if I don't want to be a doctor, Dad?"

"Oh yeah, what do you want to be?" He smiles at her. "A dentist?"

"I don't know. Maybe a vet or something."

"Or something?" He laughs and winks at me. He is beginning to lose his hair. It's thinning there at the edge of his scalp, like a cap pushed up off his head. "You be a doctor. Your daddy's a doctor and he gives you everything."

Tatay was not a doctor, and we didn't have everything. But things were different then. In our barrio, the houses had dirt floors. The bathrooms weren't always connected to the house. We didn't have running water. That was back then. During the war. Still, when we sat around the dinner table, listening to *Tatay* tell stories about the family, and what his life was like before our mother, it seemed we had everything, or so our father led us to believe.

Kuya Frank scratches his belly and stretches like a giant kitty. "This girl is beauty and brains. You know she is the reigning Miss Teenage Sampaguita?"

"Really?" I ask. "She doesn't seem the beauty queen type."

"Oh, she's as pure and innocent as the national flower. Ha, *hija?*"

"National flower?" I say. "Since when is the u.s. national flower the Sampaguita?"

"I'm really proud of her," he yells at me. Why does he shout at me, I wonder. Does he think I'm going deaf? "I give her everything. Who gave you that new car, Millicent? Daddy, right?"

She doesn't answer him. Barely looks up from what she's doing. It's as though he weren't even there.

*

After dinner, the women clear the dishes and wash the pots and pans. My brother's wife, Letty, and I exchange gossip. We haven't seen each other in a year and our big family, twelve siblings, all married and scattered throughout the United States, is always into something. It's as if *Tatay* bundled us all up in a giant mail bag and dropped us from a plane. Letty stands at the kitchen sink, rinsing and soaking, picking up dishes that Millie and I have deposited at the sink. When the table is clear and wiped clean, I stand there next to Letty, while Millie continues to dance around us. Her work is perfectly choreographed as she slips in and out of view, sometimes with a rag in her hands and sometimes with a broom.

"What about you, Millie?" I ask. "You're sixteen now, do you have a boyfriend? Do you go on dates?"

Letty looks up at me and winks. "Millie doesn't date, she has boys that are friends."

"Dad thinks I'm too young," Millie says.

"But you went to junior prom, didn't you?"

Millie waltzes around the kitchen, swishing the broom about, slipping it into the tiny crooks of the room, between the stove and the wall and the refrigerator. She glides the bristles along the floor basin. An angel.

Without looking up she says, "We just went as friends."

Letty wrings a rag and sighs. She places it onto the counter for Millie. "She's too busy for boyfriends, aren't you? What with varsity tennis and the honors program. All those 'A's."

"And let's not forget," Millie adds, "my duties as Miss Teenage Sampaguita."

Letty makes a face at her and says, "She barely has time to have a cup of tea with her mother, much less a boyfriend."

"Well, the phone must be ringing off the hook. Teenagers always have time for the telephone," I say. I pick the rag up and let it unravel in the air. It is an old white T-shirt, riddled with moth bites and other holes. I drag it across the kitchen stove's range, dig my finger into its ruts. "I know my girls are always yakking on that phone. Leonard and I are thinking of getting them their own line."

"Dad doesn't allow me to talk on the phone," Millie says. She bends down to sweep the grime into a dust pan. Her hair, long and black like midnight falls over her shoulder. "He says it's childish."

I can't tell how she feels about these things. She says them without any emotion. She's too young to date. She's too old to babble on the phone. The whole thing makes me nervous.

"*Kuya* Frank isn't that bad, is he?" I ask Letty. She looks up at me, wipes her brow with the back of her arm. Her bangs which had been combed out of her face, slip into her eyes. Like this, she is so young, not like the mother of three grown children.

"Nope," she tells me. As Millie sneaks up behind her mother and puts her arms around her waist, Letty draws her close and says, "He's worse."

"I'm just a prisoner of war, that's all," Millie whispers. She leans on Letty and kisses her.

*

Kuya Frank and I were the youngest in our family. By the time we were teenagers, *Tatay* had died of a heart attack—he was seventy. And our oldest brother was living in the United States with a family of his own. Still, he'd send us money and it was his money that put me through college and *Kuya* Frank through medical school.

Kuya Frank was never a flirt. In fact I've always imagined him to be afraid of girls. He was always very awkward around them. He kept to himself and kept a book in front of him like a face guard. He only spoke when he was spoken to and even then he would mumble.

Maybe this fear of girls is what made him so protective of me. He would follow me around campus like a guard dog, glaring at prospective suitors. I really had to work hard to ditch him back then. Thank god my oldest brother sent for him. Thank god he found him a residency program in America. I might have never met my husband.

The house is dark and *Kuya* Frank and I are sitting in front of the television, watching a late night comic spew corny jokes about President Clinton and french fries and cutting more than budgets. Ha. Ha.

"Clinton's such a joke," he tells me. "I could have predicted all this."

"Relax, *Kuya*, it's comedy." He's sitting with his feet up, reclining on one of those moving chairs, the kind that lean back electronically. He sips his beer.

"Want another?" he asks me.

I shake my head no. "I can't believe how beautiful Millie's grown."

"She looks like her mommy."

"When was the last time I saw her? Two years ago?"

On the mantle of the fireplace a small group of photos cluster around an eight-by-ten portrait of Millie. She's wearing a gown that flows from her body like a cascade of white water. Her hair has been curled up and fit into a golden crown. The sash that labels her Miss Teenage Sampaguita embroiders that name along her body in a giant red gash of lettering. Her smile, faint like a whisper, closed in an almost grimace, peels across the photo.

"So, does she like being a beauty queen?" I ask.

"Of course," he answers. "She's been in pageants since she was small. Didn't your girls ever join a contest?"

"Nope." I tell him. "They've never really shown any interest."

"Well," he says, leaning back in his chair. "You have to influence them, you know. Encourage them."

"Leonard actually did suggest it. And they both asked me about it."

"And did you tell them it was good for their reputation? That it's an honor?"

"I said it was up to them, but that for me, objectifying women like that—I don't know. It doesn't feel right." I slide my finger down the edge of the portrait's frame. Already her curves move up and out of the flounce of white fabric, flirt from underneath the gown. I can see the hint of breast, the slide of a woman's waist, sloping in and out where hips grow broad.

"That's crazy talk," he says.

"She has a sexier body than I do," I say.

"Don't talk like that."

"Well, it's true. Have you taken a look at her?"

He raises the remote and aims it at the television, pushing the volume button up and up. The laughter rises from the big-screen TV. Blue light flickers from the set and dances across his face. His face, the same one I knew when we were children, hardly different. Soft curves about the cheeks, full mouth. Sad eyes. He's always had sad eyes.

"She's only sixteen. And she's smart. She's honors all the way. I think she's going to be an excellent surgeon. She has the right kind of hands."

When I remind him that at dinner she wanted to be an animal doctor, he laughs. "She's just a kid," he says. "She doesn't know what's good for her."

I know this. I've heard it before. My brother is the fourth doctor in our house. There are four attorneys and three dentists. I'm the only one who isn't a professional. I am a mother.

"What's so great about being a doctor, *Kuya*?"

"She'll have everything this way."

"Everything we didn't have? All the things that would have made us better people? I know what you mean. We are a sorry lot, we Monteros."

"You know what I mean. She'll be somebody."

"And what about Frankie and Isabel?" His other children, the older ones, live out of the house.

"Isabel's a lost cause. She's loud and she's wild. She talks back, she will never listen to me."

"*Kuya*, she's an elementary school teacher. What's wrong with that?"

"Isabel lives in that little garage with her boyfriend. They don't even have enough money to paint the walls. What kind of life is that? She's too skinny. And Frankie is my son. He's a boy. I never needed to look at him twice."

"Raised himself, did he?"

"But Millie," he says leaning over to me and pointing his long brown finger. "Millie, is good. She's smart and she knows how to listen."

"Oh," I say, teasing him, "and she's a sexy little tropical flower, your Miss Teenage Sampaguita."

He frowns and the ends of his eyebrows meet. "She's a good girl," he says, "and she'll make a fine doctor, you'll see."

I roll my eyes at him. "I'm going to bed."

"She's the baby and she's lucky because the others grew up when we were struggling."

"Babies grow up too, *Kuya*," I tell him. I can tell he doesn't get it and I'm too tired to have to deal with this any longer. "Good night," I say. "Sweet dreams."

I leave him sitting on his recliner chair, his throne to end all thrones. The television noise gets louder as he sinks into the cushions. The house is so dark, so quiet except for that one room where the glimmering blue light moves like ocean waves and stretches out into the rooms upstairs.

*

On Saturday afternoon Isabel and Frankie boy come home from college and the family piles into *Kuya* Frank's Gold Mercedes and drives to the local church to watch Millie perform the dance of the lights.

The hall is lit by long fluorescent bulbs. The narrow wooden slats in the floor are polished and stripped of the usual basketball tape. Today there are no free throws, no dunk shots, no children's sneakers scuffing up the wooden planks. There is, instead, the Philippine bazaar.

Miss Teenage Sampaguita sits in a metal folding chair with a paperback book in her hand. She's wearing a pearl beaded *terno*, a long dress fit as a mermaid's tail with sleeves that rise high up above her shoulders, still like the broken wings of a monarch butterfly. Her hair has been swept up off her long brown neck like the photo. She reaches up to straighten the golden crown, tipped to the side of her head. It slips back. She holds her hand there, resting on the crown, and the other hand props the book up.

"Millicent," her father calls. "Shht, put that book down."

She turns the page of the book and mutters, "But I'm bored, Dad."

Kuya Frank nudges me with his elbow and pushes me towards her. "Talk some sense into her, Baby. Show her how to act like a beauty queen." He pulls the book from her and tells her, "Stop it. You're acting like a bookworm, not a beautiful flower."

"Leave her alone, Dad," Isabel says. Long as a stretch of bamboo reed, Isabel leans over to pull at his arm. Her black dress rises just above her knee, curves in and out, tracing her delicate figure. She clunks around the gym in black cowboy boots. "She said she'd do the stupid pageant; she won. What else do you want? Come on, we'll get some egg roll." Isabel's eyes dart out past the heavy liner. She smells of cinnamon and musk oil and her lips burst in burgundy reds. "*Tita* Baby," she calls to me, "you want some *lumpia* too?"

"No, Beauty," I tell her. "You two go, I'll keep Miss Teenage Sampaguita company." I slip into the chair next to her and pick up her book. "Ever seen a Sampaguita flower?" I ask Millie.

She shakes her head and stares out at the gym floor.

"When I was little," I tell her, "my mother used to take us to visit her mother's garden in Baguio. White walls enclosed my *lola's* small terrace where she grew mango trees, papaya, and gumamela. I remember this fragrance—sweet, sweet. It came from the Sampaguita flower. The tiny white petals—sort of like a daisy, but not quite—that grew on a vine and climbed the walls and the tree trunks in that garden. I guess if you grow Sampaguita next to a wall or a fence, it sort of reaches up and clings to it."

I lean back in my chair and I think of that garden. In my memory, I am a child of three or four, dressed up for Sunday. My dress is plain cotton and white with little flowers embroidered on the collar and sleeves. I remember looking up at the walls so high, I thought they crossed blue boundaries, clouds and morning stars, and I realize it wasn't just that the walls were covered with Sampaguitas; it's that they grew to be wild and abundant. It's that the white petals stretched along the walls, scaled over them, and escaped down the sides into the neighbor's yard. The fragrance filtered the air and greeted the visitors as they walked up the path to my grandmother's house. In my memory, I am alone in a corner of the garden, pulling flowers from the wall and sucking nectar from the petals and my mother and her mother, sitting on the bench under one of the mango trees, whisper to each other.

Next to me, Millie shifts in her seat. Booths line the walls and decorations of coppice shell lamps and mirrors, wicker baskets, hemp hats and placemats litter the room. "It's like a giant Filipino garage sale," she says.

As we sit there, people saunter past, calling out to her: how pretty she is, how good she is, how she must be making her parents proud. She smiles at them all; she waves. She even stands to kiss an elder or two, brings their hand up to her forehead, makes *mano*, a custom that pays respect to elders. Millie acts out her role, little miss beauty queen.

A boy, square and thick like the root of a tree, approaches the table. She rises up and gives him a hug; speaks to him quietly and sways her body into his. She lets her hips, the ones coated in beads and little pearls, kiss his. Holding the boy's hand out to me, she says, "*Tita* Baby, this is my friend, Jerry."

I stand to meet him, holding out my own hand to greet his. "Hello," I tell him. "So nice to meet you."

When he leaves, I turn to her and say, "He's the one who's just a friend."

She nods and picks up her book.

"He's cute enough," I say. "*Pogi naman ng* boyfriend *mo*."

She opens up the paperback book. "He's not my boyfriend," she says. She bends the pages of her book, a fat book where thick words and heavy black ink mark its pages.

"You're reading this?" I ask. "*War and Peace?* Whatever happened to *Go Ask Alice?*"

"Read it."

"Your daddy really loves you, Millie. He's so proud of you."

"Yeah," she answers as she grabs the book from me. "That's what he says."

"Oh but he does. See how hard he works for you and how he shows you off?"

Millie folds the book gently, and places it on her lap. Looking up at me she smiles. "*Tita*, you haven't been around long enough to see how hard Daddy works. He's always making rounds or in surgery or at his office. On Wednesdays and weekends he's on the golf course. He works real hard."

"For you, *hija*," I tell her, brushing a stray hair from her forehead. "I mean all he does is talk about your accomplishments. Frankly, it gets kind of boring."

"Yup. I'll say. Ask him about my last tennis tournament. Ask him what the match point looked like. He's got it on video. He asked coach's kid to tape it for him."

She flips through the book, reading and rereading the pages. She turns her head away from me, a quiet flower with a scent so faint, so sweet, I think I must be imagining it. And before I can say anything else, she mouths the words to the book. Engrossed, she hears nothing else.

*

We sit in a dark auditorium and wait. The rattle of canned mandolin and a twelve-string guitar announce the dance of lights. The crowd, which has been talking loudly among themselves, sobers up, waiting. They hold their breath as a train of twelve candles, disembodied and floating, travels across the floor.

"Isabel," Frankie junior hisses. "How come Dad never made you do this?"

"Ever hear of the word no?" she whispers. "She's such a little wimp."

"Enough," *Kuya* Frank warns them.

Sitting in the dark like that, the solitary flicker of candles and what could be moonlight only draws attention to their voices, everyone listens. I hold my breath, nervous for Millie, who cannot speak up or tell her siblings to shut up. I wonder if she can hear them.

The lights begin to sway, to move in circular motions, to rise up high next to the young faces of the Teenage dancers. Millicent, like a beam of light, hovers in the center of the circle, moves in the glimmer of candlelight. There is something magical about her face, the way her eyes travel beyond the dark, far far away, travel across the gym and up through the skylights.

She never smiles. She doesn't laugh like the other girls. Someone stumbles and the concentration is lost for a moment in all their faces, in all but Millie's. She keeps her mouth closed, hides her braces like her feelings.

*

Out in the church parking lot, just underneath the old maple tree, I pull out a cigarette and light it. I drink in the night and the vapors of nicotine. Holding my breath, my arms wrapped tightly around my body, I let the smoke fill me up and then I release. The smoke wafts its way into the black suburban sky, threads itself up and out into the universe. I imagine my breath floating as high as the planets, weaving its way around the constellations, on its way to God. Stars dot the horizon and flash so brightly, I think there must be a coded message coming from them. What, I wonder. What are you saying? I take another long slow drag.

"Smoking? You know that's bad, Baby."

God, it's that voice, I think. Why can't I walk away from it? I exhale and watch the fog rise and tangle its way up into the boughs of the maple tree. "It relaxes me," I answer.

"I thought I broke you of that habit long ago."

Kuya Frank walks across the parking lot, zig-zagging between bumpers and the tops of minivans. "What happens if you get lung cancer, huh, Baby?"

"What happens if you're hit by a truck?" I answer. "It's all relative."

"So how's Leonard?" he asks. He drags his feet and the gravel below him rumbles louder and louder as he nears.

"You should know," I tell him. "Didn't I hear you talking to him on the phone tonight?"

"What are you doing here, Baby? Your children are home taking care of their father. He's confused. What are you doing?"

"I'm visiting my older brother. What are you doing calling my house behind my back?"

In the moonlight, his eyes shine bright like those nights we'd sneak out of the house to fish in monsoon-swollen rivers. He smiles and the dimple in the cleft of his chin deepens. "You have responsibilities, Baby. You can't just leave."

It's as if the sun has come out. I feel the heat spreading, starting from my belly and rising, reaching the cavity of my chest, the limbs—arms and legs, and up through my throat. My face is hot. Red. "First of all, *Kuya*, you don't know what's going on because I haven't told you. Secondly, this is my business."

"This is not a hotel, and you are not a visitor. You're staying with me, and I'm your brother."

"And if you love me, you'll let me do what I need to do. Don't worry. I'm working this out." I tug at his sleeve and punctuate the end of this conversation.

A cool breeze winds its way around the tree's limbs, pours down on us, brushes my skirt so it floats a little. And then he tells me, "You're not a girl anymore, you're a grown woman."

"Are you deaf? I told you to drop it." A wind brushes my skirt up and I slap it back down with my arm. The tip of my cigarette burns a hole in the fabric. "*Puñeta*," I swear under my breath. What I want to do is shake him. He hasn't changed at all. He makes me nuts and it's as though we are twelve and fifteen all over again, or twenty-five and twenty-seven or six and eight. "For once you're right, I am a grown woman. Now leave me alone." I put the cigarette up to my lips and tug the air right out of it. He snatches it from me and throws it out into the lot.

"You're still stubborn. You haven't changed," he says. And turning, he walks away. "Come on," he tells me. "We're going home."

*

Sometimes when you are the baby, there really is no way out. There is no such thing as no, even though you know this hell, this place your family makes you go to dwell, smothers you like death itself. Sometimes, when you're the baby of so many, you're lucky they remember you long enough to tell you what to do, so you don't make a fuss. You just do it. No one ever asks you what you want. Sometimes when you're it, and choices are left to the older ones, you take what you can and you stop harboring dreams of your own. It's easier than fighting. And easier than covering up that disappointment that comes with being forgotten. It's less work, letting your *tatay* and your brothers and sisters and your mother and all the aunties, uncles, and *lola*s run your life, poke into what was once yours. At least, that's what I remember from being the baby. No escape. And so when I see her fetching water for her father and when I see her perusing medical school catalogs when she isn't even out of high school, I get a little claustrophobic. Why doesn't she say no? Why doesn't she speak up? Why am I so upset?

I read the Sunday morning paper while Millie sets up the coffee maker. She pours espresso beans from the canister to the grinder, brushing sleep from her eyes with the back of her free hand. Sometimes she really does look like a baby, dressed in an oversized white T-shirt, her cocoa-brown legs sticking straight out like two little twigs. After sleep her face is full, slightly swollen with youth and the unrequired slumber that comes with being a Teenager.

"So you want to take care of animals?" I ask her. "Here's a want ad." I lift the paper up, its pages floating in the air like wings. "They're looking for volunteers at the shelter. Have you ever done that?"

She shakes her head, lazily turns the water faucet on and fills the pot. "Dad won't let me get a job. I have to study."

"Oh, honey, but this isn't a job—it's volunteer work. You can get experience and see if being a vet is what you really want."

"Thanks, *Tita* Baby," she says leaning over to kiss my cheek. "I probably won't be a pet doc."

"I thought you said you wanted that."

"Maybe. But the truth is, if having a career and being a doctor—for people or animals—means you're never home, I don't think I want it. I mean, what I want is a family and how can you do that if you're never around?" She stops moving. Standing at the island in the middle of the kitchen, the morning sun rings her body like a giant halo and soaks right through the bones of her delicate frame. "I mean if I have a family, I want to hang out with my kids. Know them." She speaks in a small voice, one that falters and stops short of breath.

"Millie," I tell her. I put my arms out to her. "Come here." I draw her towards me. "You're only sixteen. You don't have to know what you're going to do for the rest of your life." When I get close, I see tears scatter across the landscape of her face and color her eyes and mouth sweetly, sadly. "You know they call me Baby—right? My real name's Rosaria. Who calls me Rosaria? No one, not even you. I'm *Tita* Baby. You can't imagine how it was for me. Twelve older brothers and sisters. All very smart. Your grandfather was so strict. Lecturing us, always lecturing us. And when he died and all the other brothers and sisters were here in the States and I was left alone with your grandmother and father—my god. Your father—who is only two years older than me, registered me for college and picked out all my courses. I was twenty-five and still he wouldn't let me go on dates without a chaperon. He wanted me to be a nurse. Can you imagine? And he's only my brother. When I came to America it was even worse, because then everyone was telling me what to do. Your *lola* and I used to scream at each other."

"That's why you eloped?" She runs her hand along my back, as if I am the one in need of comfort. "It's why you ran away?"

"Millie, I am forty-two years old, and my brothers and sisters are still trying to tell me how to live. They think they can tell me how to raise my family, how to cook rice, even how to dress, and I'm a grown woman. Look, even your dad. Since I've arrived all he does is lecture me. Like he knows what it's like to be a wife and mother."

"He's good at that, huh? Lecturing, I mean." She looks down and her hair falls about her face and hides it. She unravels a thread in her T-shirt, pulls at it, twists hard to break it free and says, "All I want is to be left alone. No—I mean I wish he wasn't always showing me a way to be better. It's that or he buys me things. Remember how he brought up that car? I'd rather play tennis or watch TV with him."

I try to explain it to her. Try to show her how the difficult times in the Philippines—like hiding from soldiers, American and Japanese; or surviving seasons when typhoons destroyed our rice paddies; or wearing a shirt ten times a hand-me-down, a shirt so worn, there was nothing left, but a T-shirt with holes; how all that made her father crazy. "He doesn't want you to ever want. He wants to make sure you are provided for, *hija*." I try to tell her it's out of love, but even I can't help wondering why he's so ruthless. So I say, "Isabel talks back."

Millie rolls her eyes. "They used to fight all the time and then one day my dad just gave up."

"You can't talk back, you're like me. Have you tried reasoning with him?"

"We're talking about my father, remember? I get straight 'A's and he still nags me about studying."

Her stories fill me up. Start from the bottom of my soles and rise high into my throat. Her stories wring my insides and my heart and I find myself choking. What is she going to do? What am I going to do? When I could no longer beat my voice against his soundproof heart, I packed one suitcase and I was gone. When my voice felt so small, when it finally disappeared and I knew there was no point, I left. Actions speak louder than words, I told myself.

"I'm not saying you should disobey your father," I say.

"I know, and the thing is, I really do love him."

I know that too. And her mother, like my mother, like myself, our voices are so small sometimes, and the work that must get done is so interminable. And what I hate most of all is seeing her, Miss

Teenage Sampaguita, withering like the rest of us. Growing faint. Dying like white petals fraying from the vine, and slipping silently from walls and fences, and falling like compost onto fertile ground.

FILMING SAUSAGE

Day One of Nine

The assistant director, Bud, welcomes you with a huge hug. You have never met him before. He gives you the materials you need to keep the continuity on this job: a script, the storyboards, a shooting schedule. You're to make sure that each camera shot is legal—that clothes are exactly the same for each take, sleeves rolled three-quarters up each time, hair parted on the camera right side, every time. You will see to it that the plates have three Danny Boy sausages, one with a bite, the other two pointing camera left, every time. You watch the details in the spot. You keep the director honest.

"Why don't you get settled—grab something to eat," Bud tells you, "then I'll introduce you to Dick, he's the director."

The craft service table is in the backyard, under the shade of a hundred year old maple tree. To get there you must weave your body around the cables and giant lights which sit cold on the lawn of this house. Wave to some of the guys hauling lights from the truck. "Hey Tom! Solly! How ya doin' Mike?" They look up and call your name, grunt hello while you crawl beneath the scaffolding.

Your friend Katy drags two different kinds of rocking chairs around the corner of the house, "Elena!" she calls. "How are you?"

Standing at craft service where there is always something to graze on—bagels and cheese, chocolate donuts and ham sandwiches on white, you coddle a hot cup of coffee. Jump out of the way of a toddler as he runs about your legs chasing a man in a jean jacket and baseball cap. The man dodges the boy, pretends to be scared of him, then turns about to capture the child and nibble at his belly. The boy laughs and mutters, "Daddy, daddy, oh daddy!" You smile at them. It's nice, you think, to see a father and son in love like this. Imagine your boyfriend, Aaron, imagine a son and think you'd like this someday too. A small woman peeks around the tree and approaches the two. "Okay, Samuel," she says. "That's enough. Daddy has to work now." She takes the boy from the man and balances the child on her narrow hip.

After your coffee, Bud ushers you into the house, holding his palm to the small of your back. Wriggle ahead of him. He doesn't seem to notice this and places his hand on your shoulder, leading you to a room that's cramped with lights and sound blankets, teeming with grips, prop people, account execs from Harbor, Conahan and Lunt. Already the air is hot and stale inside the house; already it smells of sweat and burning rubber and it's only seven-thirty in the morning.

"Dick," Bud calls. "This is your script and continuity, Elena." Bud holds his arm out to Dick Reinhonker. Reinhonker stands tall and skinny like a newly sharpened pencil. He has salt and pepper hair which recedes from his forehead, slipping quietly underneath a baseball cap turned backward. His sparse beard runs along the edge of his face, linking his sideburns to one another. He has brown eyes that are wide and laugh lines that crease nicely as he welcomes you. He puts his hand out and draws you to him. "Nice to meet you," he says.

Say, "That's quite a little boy you have."

"Samuel—he's a little monster all right. I'm Dick." He offers you his hand. "Ellen?"

"Elena," you tell him. "Elena Romero."

He wants to know where you are from, so you tell him Ann Arbor.

A production assistant approaches the two of you. She carries a cup of coffee and a donut. She holds it out to Dick, says, "I have some more hidden in the back."

He takes the offering from her, kisses her thanks and you gather this was his special request—grape jelly donuts. He turns back to you and asks again, "Where are you from?" You're used to people asking you this question and never being satisfied when you answer, Ann Arbor, but this really is where you're from. You know he wants to know the history of your black hair, the brown in your skin, the almond of your eyes, but you will not give in. You like to make people work for this answer. You enjoy seeing them squirm, but Dick doesn't squirm. Instead he laughs and says, "And where are your people from, Elena?"

"My people? You mean my ethnicity?"

"You're quick," he laughs as he brushes the hair off your forehead. "You'll keep me honest, won't you? " He winks at you then and you laugh.

The two of you find a corner in the house and begin to review the spots. You will be shooting three commercials in nine days, he tells you. Long days.

"I know this sounds a bit sick," Dick says as he pages through the script, "but what the agency wants us to do is to send out the message that America is sausage in the morning, sunrise at the farm, spicy pork links, grandma, and love." He looks at you, smiling, his eyes friendly as a puppy dog. "What do you think, Ellen, sick?"

Smile back at him, say, "Elena."

Dick tells you that he is going to rely on you. "I need to know what comes before the shot, and then what comes after it. Continuity is important on this one."

You think that you will like working with him okay, he seems nice enough, if only he'd get your name right. You imagine that in his youth, he was probably attractive.

The first shot is of an elderly woman named Bel Moss who's dressed in a gingham checkered apron. She has blond-white hair and light blue eyes. She stands at a kitchen stove, one that Katy rented from Period Prop Rentals, and stirs a pan of Danny Boy sausages.

The camera is set upon a dolly, a giant tripod on wheels which holds not only the camera, but the director and you. Underneath the actual camera, Dick wraps his hands about two metal wheels—one at the back of the camera's neck, and one to the left of the camera. He guides which way the camera floats, spinning the metal wheel much like a sailor would at sea. You sit at the back of the dolly, notebook on your lap, pens in your hands. Label your notes "Day One of Nine." Around your neck, wear two digital stopwatches that glow in the dark. Use these to count the seconds, the tenths of seconds.

The house is slowly quieting as everyone finds a place to sit. The grips walk out into the yard to smoke a cigarette or have another cup of coffee. They've lit the kitchen, made it warm and cozy, created that loving feeling. Katy tiptoes about the set, carrying a cloth diaper in her hand and occasionally wiping a smudge off the counter, the refrigerator, the toaster oven. The only voice that can be heard now is Dick's. He tells Bel to stir the sausages counterclockwise—"It's more appealing," he says. Bel follows directions well when she can hear them. Her hearing isn't so good. He is tilting the camera from the frying pan to her face and it is important that she smile on cue. You will count three seconds out and she will smile on three and sigh, "Danny Boy," on four. Bud struts circles about the camera dolly, heaving his jeans up to his swollen belly as Dick squints into the camera's eye piece. Dick mutters, "Yes, yes, yes in a minute. Hold on."

"Let's shoot this baby," Bud tells him. "We gotta go." He tap dances in place and then asks, "Ready?" Dick nods. Bud turns to face the rest of the crew and calls out "That's it! Close it up and keep it down!"

Call out, "Scene One-oh-One take one is up!" and a series of voices—the assistant camera, video, and sound—acknowledge you as each one repeats, "One-oh-one, take one."

Bud rattles off a chain of commands, "Roll sound, roll camera, speed!" Dick looks over his shoulder, smiles at you, winks and says, "Let's ride this baby." When he's not looking, roll your eyes. Finally Dick calls out to Bel, "Action!"

Bel misses her cue. "Damn," Dick whispers after the twenty-seventh take. Though she can't hear him, Bel senses his hostility and she drops the frying pan on the floor, splattering grease on her one-of-a-kind apron. "It's okay sweetie, it's okay," he tells Bel, as he climbs down from the camera dolly. To you he says, "Let's look at what we've got."

Jump off the dolly, carting your pens and pad. The stopwatch-es swing across your breasts as you chase after Dick. Walk past his wife, who is standing behind the clients. Smile and say hello. She's looking right at you, but doesn't bother answering. Dick's strides are long and he is hard to keep up with. You hop over boxes and cables, trying not to trip, trying desperately to hear what he is saying. He is fast and unaware of how closely you trail him.

"The first nineteen were no good," you tell him. "You said they 'sucked egg.' You liked take twenty and twenty-two. You said take twenty-five was 'Awesome for action, shaky on camera'."

He says, "You write down everything I say?"

"Verbatim," you tell him. "I figure writing down what you say will jog your memory—help you look for certain things."

"What if I don't mean it?" he asks.

"Mean what?"

"The stuff I say, what if it's all bullshit and you write it down?"

"Then you'll have to keep track of what you mean and what you don't mean. I just write what I hear."

He smiles at you and nudges your arm. "You're good. Not only beautiful, but smart too."

Stand with your back straight, not lilting to his touch, not recoiling either. Stand perfectly still. Turn your attention to your work. Your notes are detailed color coded messages. You know you are good at this, that editors love to get your notes because they are clear and to the point. Write down that the first shot was shot at eight-ten. Circle the takes that Dick liked. Put a triangle around the ones the client liked.

A dozen agency people huddle around Dick. Remain just outside their circle. The men wear baggy pants with teal-blue and burgundy shirts, loud ties and tennis shoes. The women have on heavy eye makeup and blush. Their lips are lined with red pencil—they wear expensive sweaters and pant suits, red leather miniskirts and white blouses with leather ties to match. They sit in front of the monitor with their yellow note pads and wind up toys. "She's perfect, she's beautiful," they're saying. "We love when she smiles like she's going to cry."

"Yeah, yeah, like the thought of her grandson coming home moves her to tears."

"Yeah," Dick says. "You know, I work with a lot of old people and she's one of the best. She's right on."

"There's one take that we just loved" says a man. "Which was it, Kerrie?"

Kerrie, one of the women in red leather, snaps her fingers, says, "Oh yeah, it was, it was . . . which one was it?"

"You liked take twenty-one," you remind her. Look up at Dick, he's smiling at you, nodding.

"You can hear from all the way over there?" he asks.

Say, "Of course."

You all watch take twenty-one in playback, a take that Dick had labeled "Fucked up" and the agency people say—"See how her lips tremble like that? Beautiful."

"Circle that take," Dick tells you. "It's a beauty, a true keeper."

He turns to run back to the camera and you follow him. He smiles and reaches out to you, wraps your shoulders with his arm and says, "Well, Ellen, looks like we fooled them."

When Bel comes back on set, she has on different glasses. "Are those the ones you normally wear?" you ask.

"Oh dear, I forgot my prop glasses," she sighs. Dick taps your shoulders, says, "Good call, Ellen, good call." Remind him that your name is not Ellen, it's Elena and he grins at you and says, "Whatever."

Katy walks up to the camera, carrying two footstools—one is hand-carved with little hearts at the legs and the other is plain and painted white. She holds them up to Dick and says, "Which one, Dick?" She winks at you.

"That's for the porch?" he asks.

"Uh-huh." She holds the white one up and says, "This one doesn't match the rocking chairs, but it looks good on the porch. The other one is grandma-like and matches the chair."

"That one," Dick says as he points to the white stool.

Katy turns to leave, but he calls her back. "Come here," he says. He puts his arms around Katy's waist and she returns his hug. "You're doing a wonderful job, Katy."

"For you, Dick," she says laughing, "anything."

When Katy walks away, Dick turns to you. Look past him to the set up in the kitchen. He says, "So, you and Katy friends?"

Tell him you are. He watches you out of the corner of his eye and whispers, "Really?" Look at him, confused, almost ask, "What do you mean by that?" but don't.

At lunch, Bud tells you that Dick's impressed. "He likes you." Bud says, "He never likes script supervisors."

Letty, the wardrobe lady from L.A. who reads peoples palms in between the filming, whispers, "Oh honey, that's because he has a thing for Asian women."

Say, "I'm not Asian, I'm American."

She laughs and lifting your hand up to the light, she runs her fingers along the creases of your palm. Smile at her. Say, "Well, Filipina American, really." You are glib because you have heard this joke too many times for you to react—that you are all alike, that you are all exotic, that there are men in this world who are into "Asian" women. You used to get worked up over this. You used to despise men like that. Now you are too old to care. The

Mata Haris of this world are in the movies, not making them as you are. And that is the woman those men seek, not you.

"Yes," Letty hums. "Your lines are strong. You are stubborn. Know what you want. You will live a very very long life, honey. I mean it honey, you will."

Just then the woman from this morning walks into the room, carrying the toddler. Everybody stands to greet her.

"What's her name?" you ask.

"Keiko," Letty says. Keiko's hair is not exactly black—actually it looks a little like it's supposed to be, but some dye job contaminated the color and now it's more like black and red. Her skin is olive and her eyes are brown. "She's not Asian either," Letty laughs. "Right." Samuel's screaming, "Daddy!" He reaches out his arms to Dick and dives right out of Keiko's arms.

"Hey Samuel, what's up dude?" Dick says. He rubs his beard across the child's face, tickles him, kisses.

"They travel with him on all his jobs. Before Chicago, they were with us in Seattle," Letty informs you. "Before that, Toronto."

Say, "That's nice. I mean, that she can take off like that to be with her husband."

"Yeah," Letty says, blowing smoke out from her nostrils. "Suppose it's a way of keeping an eye on him."

Keiko wraps herself around Dick's long torso, whispers in his ear. Her hair falls back and exposes the white line of her neck. "She's pretty," you say. Letty laughs cynically.

That night, Dick asks you to come out with him and Bud and a few of the clients—to discuss the next day's shooting schedule, he says. To make sure you're all working like a team. Because you are not really being asked, but being told, you accompany them to dinner. Dick tells you to have anything you want, "It's on the company," he says. Order a plate of grilled calamari and a rich salmon linguini. Have two glasses of wine. Enjoy your meal, but not the company. This is part of your job, to sit with these people and talk about ways to shoot sexy sausages and eggs. You think it's strange that other than Bud and Katy, you are the only one from the crew, but the meeting's at an Italian restaurant, and you love eating Italian.

Finish work at midnight. When you arrive at home, sit at the foot of the bed and watch your boyfriend Aaron sleep. It's dark and all you really see is his shadow—but you imagine the look on his face, a slight smile, dark lashes, the angle of his chin. He's curled up like an infant which makes you want to crawl alongside him, rest next to him. He reaches, pulling you to him and whispers, "Long day, huh?"

Mold your body into his and sigh. Lots of the guys are on the job, tell him, Solly, Jeff, Andy, even Katy. Tell him that the director insisted you attend the pre-pro meeting. Say it wasn't bad. "The food was good," you tell him. "And I was on double-time."

Aaron wants to know what the director's like. Say, "He has a thing for Asian women."

"Not that," he sighs. "I hate that."

Close your eyes and try to stop thinking. For a while, the day flutters past your lids, rolling out like a series of unfinished scenes, until your mind, like the rest of you, slips under the covers and sleeps.

Day Two of Nine

Tell Bud that Dick has rearranged the shooting schedule. Show which shots have been canceled. Dick crossed them off the storyboards himself. "He doesn't think we need them," you say. "He's trying to buy time for that one shot, at sunrise, the one in the field with the cows."

When Dick arrives he kisses every one hello. Someone brings him a cup of coffee and a grape jelly donut. Dick reaches out for you and tells you that you look great today. He uses the word "hot." Smile at him uncomfortably. When you back away, he moves in even closer, brushes your shoulder with his. "Are those really your legs?"

You're standing against the house, wearing black leggings with a baggy sweater. You're wearing boots that climb your legs, hit past the tops of your knees. Your notebook rests on your hip as you finger the buttons on your stopwatch. Not sure if he's joking or what, ignore him.

He reaches out to graze the top of your thigh with the tip of his finger. Back away. Don't let him touch you. Decide he's joking. Say, "No, Dick, these are not my legs. I borrowed them from props."

He smirks out loud. You feel his laughter rolling into your ear like morning fog off a summer lake. "Kidder," he whispers. Dick tosses this empty, awkward moment at you like an NBA basketball and somehow you miss the toss, let the ball hit your hands and dribble down the side of you. He smiles as if to say, "Two points." Then he calls out to Katy, "Come here, Katy my dear, and tell me how things are going."

Katy puts her arms around Dick's waist, tells him that things are going just swell. Look at them and sigh, think maybe it's time for more coffee and walk away. Dick calls to you, and so you turn to see him kissing Katy on the cheek. "Could you bring back a cup for me?" he asks. Shudder.

The first shot for today is of a man driving a black Saab. He races up a dirt road at dawn, drives past a flurry of chickens, a corral full of dairy cows. He's coming home. The prodigal son. The country boy gone city. The assistant camera person rattles off a list of filters—colors that will enhance the homecoming—corals and pinks, reds and ambers. The crew works together to achieve this sincere moment. Dick approaches from behind, kisses your cheek and laughing, asks, "Are you teaching her camera techniques, Joe?"

"Elena's the one keeping me on my toes—did you want a Coral-grad-one or was it a Coral-grad-two?"

"I wanted two," Dick says. "I want it to be rich."

"See?" You wink at Joe. "Told you."

"This girl knows what she's doing, Joe," Dick says as his palm rubs the back of your neck. Though his hand is warm, you shiver coldly, feel goose bumps rise in your arms. "She scares me."

"I'm not supposed to scare you, Dick," you say as you step away from him. "I'm supposed to make you feel better."

"Oh?" His eyes widen and you can feel a flush of red color your face like a filter out of Joe's kit.

"I mean, with me around you're not supposed to worry about these details."

He leans into you—brushes your forehead with a kiss. Laugh nervously. Say nothing. This will pass. Think of your mother—she would frown if she knew that people were so casual about touching her daughter at work. She'd frown at men and women behaving this way in public. It means nothing, you whisper to your mom as if she were next to you, it's just the way they are in this business. Everyone does it and you know that for the most part, so do you. You have to.

The camera dolly has been placed at the edge of a farmer's driveway. As you wait for the sun to create that homecoming moment, sit on the dolly and count out the length of the shot. Hit the button on the stopwatch and read: "Working in the city made breakfast a thing of the past. I never had time for anything more than coffee . . ." Sit with your legs crossed at the edge of the dolly, mumbling the copy to yourself, timing and re-timing the words that run about ten seconds. Every now and then, you look up to see what the rest of the crew is doing. Mostly they run about, scattered across the field between the camera and the house, hauling large pieces of scaffolding. Dick sits in a high-backed director's chair, drinking coffee with a little kick as Bud circles him, talks at him. Twice you look up and Dick is staring at you. Ignore him. Don't blow your top. You need to get along. Go back to the script, but he is getting on your nerves and you begin to shake your leg, swing it off the dolly. "What?" you finally ask him, "What?"

He grins and says, "Nothing, Elena, just looking."

Slam your notebook shut and walk away. Maybe it's you. You're being too sensitive. Think about your niece Amanda who knows an imaginary person named Roy. According to Amanda, Roy makes mud cookies and feeds them to her dolls—dirties them, undresses them, and pulls out their hair. Of course you know it's Amanda baking mud pies—not Roy. No one believes the child when she blames Roy. You want to think of a way to bring up this uncomfortable feeling, you want to tell on Dick, the way she tells on Roy, but who would you tell? What would you say?

An hour passes. The light filters over the horizon and the man in the car drives into the camera's point of view. Just as he begins to pass the chicken coop, the animal wrangler who is stooped underneath the hen house wiggles an invisible prod and the chickens dance into the camera's frame on cue. The city boy pulls up to the farm house just as Bel's supposed to come onto the porch with her plate of sausages. Bud yells into a walkie talkie "Action." This is Bel's cue, but no one comes through the door. "Action," he calls again and still there is no movement.

"God damn it!" yells Dick. "What the hell's happening in there?"

Shoot this scene fifty-five times. The sun rises fast into the sky and that magic moment's lost. The clients from Harbor, Conahan and Lunt sit behind the camera dolly, whispering to themselves words so small you can barely make them out. Write down, "Clients brood over shot. Look a bit worried." The crickets have stopped chirping, and Dick and Bud are pacing the fields, arguing one hundred yards away.

Remind both Bud and Dick of the shots Dick has eliminated, assure them that they're not behind when they consider this, but Dick explodes, "Who said we're not shooting those shots? We have to! Who says we can buy time? Impossible."

Step away from Dick, toss a look at Bud who runs his palm up and down the stretch of his face. Show Dick your notes, show him where he's crossed shots off the list himself. He looks at you and says —"Why do you write everything down? Everything I say? Stop that. You have to stop that." He turns away from you, storms across the open field, screams at you, "Write this down,

Dick is always right, he's the director!"

Keiko brings their son, Samuel, to location during lunch. She sits at a table conversing with Letty, smoking a cigarette while she pokes at a salad. She drinks seltzer water from a bottle and watches Dick and Samuel strut around the set with Bud. Samuel rides on his father's shoulders, laughing as he tugs at Dick's gray wisps. They are singing the song, "I've Been Working on the Railroad."

At a table with Katy and some of the grips, finish the last of an apple cobbler doused in a melting mound of vanilla ice cream.

"I don't know how you all put up with him," Solly says.

"Well," Katy says, "it's just not worth getting worked up over." Katy drapes her arms across two folding chairs making her look like a scarecrow dressed in some man's hand-me-down clothes. Her blonde hair is piled high up on her head like an empty hornet's nest. She winks at you says, "Right, Elena? Not worth it."

Look across at Keiko who is watching her husband and child. She is waving at them when she catches you looking at her. You nod your head at Keiko and smile. In return, she looks away, tosses her head back at your table and blows a heavy dose of smoke from her red lips.

That night, Aaron cooks *pancit*, stir-fry vegetables and chicken with noodles.

"Where'd you learn to cook *pancit?*" you ask him.

"Your *lola*," he answers as he heaps the noodles onto your plates.

"What, you called my grandmother? Aaron, this is my favorite." Lean over and kiss him, rub his back. "I can't believe you did this."

"This job's a rough one," he tells you. "I wanted to make something that would help you get through it. Then I remembered how your family always makes *pancit* on birthdays," he says. "So, I called your *lola* and asked her for the recipe for —"

"Long life noodles!" you say laughing. Look into Aaron's face and carve the lines of his smile with the edge of your finger.

"You're such a modern guy," tell him. Feel the tears rising up inside you, you are so tired. "What did *Lola* say?"

"She said next time she'd teach me how to make fresh egg rolls and she wanted to know why don't you just tell that guy off."

"You know why." Tell Aaron that half the time you don't know what Dick means—is he joking, is he serious? Is he coming on to you? What? Sometimes he's nice. Sometimes he's charming.

"Charming?" Aaron asks.

"Well, with his son, he's charming, other times he's just sleazy."

Day Three of Nine

Today you are shooting more interiors of the kitchen. Walk around the set snapping Polaroid pictures for continuity. Walk around with your notebook and mark the little things—the sugar bowl's position, the time on the kitchen clock, the angle of the table to the lens. Dick follows you, says, "I feel like you don't like me, Ellen. Do you?"

When he looks at you, you feel like the gaffer has turned the lights on you—your face gets hot and you can feel the perspiration seeping from the pores of your skin. He grabs onto your arm and turns you to him. He is waiting for an answer. "Elena, do you like me?"

Ignore him. Turn away. Walk over to the camera dolly and look at the markings on the camera—a ten-to-one zoom lens, no filters, roll number ten.

He sneaks up behind you, whispers, "You know, Ellen, you're not being honest with me. I like my script girls to be honest." Walk to the back of the dolly. Though your instinct is to lash out, say you are not a script girl, you're a script supervisor and you are not HIS script supervisor, you are not his anything, you say nothing. Feel him standing next to you, his shadow creeping over you. Scribble into your note book, hear him tell you to add to your notes some obscenity—the obscenity for day three. Walk up to Bud, say, "I'm stepping off set for a minute."

As you walk away Dick yells after you, "Something the matter?"

Later, your face is buried in your notes, but you feel another's presence. You feel someone almost touching you, seeing right into you and you feel naked. Continue to look down at your notes. Flip the pages of the script, run your fingers along the storyboard. Dive into the pages of your notes, scribbling things you will remind Dick of later on.

Finally look up, as you continue to write. Dick is staring at you and his eyes, the ones that were warm like that puppy dog's have grown dark and sullen. Possessed, you think. "Always writing little notes. Got the world on a note pad. Here," he whispers as he leans into you, breathing words onto the nape of your neck, "write this down: suck director's dick after wrap."

Squirm forward, dropping several pens and markers from your pouch. Reaching down, you pick them up, move away from Dick. Your notes go flying—the script, the storyboard. Katy runs over to help you pick up the papers before they blow about.

"My God, you're still a klutz," she says laughing. "Ever since I've known you, Elena, you've been a hazard on the set."

She hands you your papers and as you take them, she squeezes your hand and smiles.

There are six days left, after today. You think you can put up with Dick just long enough to do the job and take your pay check. Scribble down his words. Write them big and dark. They appear heavy on the page. Note the time.

Day Four of Nine

At five in the morning, the production company closes down LaSalle, a boulevard that leads right to Chicago's Board of Trade. The sky reflects blue/black against a moon that still shines white light, a light which contrasts with bright copper street lamps along the avenue. The street is wide and empty and lined on either side with tall granite buildings. The shot will be of the man in the Saab sitting in the middle of morning rush hour traffic. His black Saab is stuck between a city bus and a chauffeur-driven limo. A yellow cab cuts him off. A bike messenger swerves into his lane. None of this helps his attitude—he's grumpy, which makes him remember he's hungry, which leads him to fantasize about going home for a good breakfast, home to Grandma O'Connor and Danny Boy Sausages.

The police have blocked off the streets while Bud directs prop-car drivers into appropriate lanes to create a controlled rush hour environment. Several production assistants line the sidewalks, guiding extras to walk past the camera on cue. The crew is setting up to shoot at sunrise.

Wrapped in a down coat, you stand alongside of the camera, next to Dick, jumping up on your toes to keep warm. He tells you, "Remind me that I want to get an extreme close-up of his hands hitting the horn, and remind me not to forget to get both a hand-held shot and a steady camera shot from in the car looking out. Oh—and I want to get close-ups of other drivers too for cut-aways."

Still jogging in place, you keep your hands deep in your pockets, nod your head up and down. He looks at you and smiles. "So Asia," he says. Asia, like the continent, like the band.

"Elena."

"I'm the director, Asia, I can call you anything I want. Anyhow, are you going to remember all those reminders or are you going to put them into that pad of yours?"

Jot down, "Remind Dick." At five A.M. it's cold and though it's only October, you're wearing knit gloves. You've cut the fingers off like a pauper kid, so your fingers can move freely between the buttons of your stopwatch, the pen, and the pages.

"How many rolls of film have we shot so far?" he asks. You tell him seventeen rolls at four thousand feet a roll. He nods his head then turns away from you. Follow him into the trailer where the actor is getting dressed.

The motor home is crowded with clients. They are looking at ties—paisley, polka-dots, stripes and flowers. Wide ties, bow ties, narrow leather ties. They look at navy, reds, teals, and burgundy and bright yellows with purple accents.

"What do you think, Dick?" Kerrie asks. "We want our country boy to look powerful and yet not snobbish, rich but still down home."

"We want him to read 'America' and 'Danny Boy Sausage' at once," says a man in a Hawaiian shirt, baseball cap and trenchcoat.

"What do you think, Asia?" Dick asks you. Glance about the motor home, see people picking at their clothing, scribbling into note pads, trying not to catch your eye. "Navy and red striped, don't you think?" No one is speaking. There is only the hum of the motor home engine. You know that they are waiting for you, waiting to see what you will do.

Say nothing. Pretend you haven't heard him. Open your notes to yesterday and say, "Yesterday, you all thought that navy/red stripes would be too obvious. You narrowed it down to the teal and burgundy paisley and the navy with white pin-point polka-dots." Say this to the group of clients, completely aware that Dick is looking at you with his brows ruffled together like the feathers of an angry bird.

When you leave the trailer walk ahead of Dick. March back to the camera which stands at the end of the block. Dick calls out to you, "Hey, Asia!"

Keep walking. "Asia, come back here!" he yells. "I'm talking to you! Answer me when I speak to you!"

When you get to the camera, look at Bud who is hunched over with his hands in his down vest, blowing smoke from his mouth into the air. Next to him stands Keiko in an oversized parka, smoking another cigarette. When Bud sees you his eyebrows rise, ready to greet you, but you beat him to it and say, "Hi Bud, Dick wants you to check with weather one more time."

"Okee," he says, leaving you two alone. Turn to Keiko. "We haven't been introduced," tell her, "but my name is Elena." She looks at you and says, "I know." Tell her that you admire her for being such a dedicated wife, dedicated mother. Tell her you couldn't do what she's doing.

"Oh well," Keiko says. Her voice is thick with a Japanese accent. "He's my husband and Sammy's father. We go where he goes." Look at the roots of her hair, they're dark and mis-colored, awkward as snow on the beaches of Hawaii. You want to advise her, "Don't follow him, leave him." Instead say, "You must love him very much."

As the two of you stand there, watch Dick at the end of the block. See him shifting on his feet, staring. She looks towards Dick too and after awhile Keiko turns to you and says, "It's not so hard." Her eyes are wet and you aren't sure if it's from the chill in the air or if she's crying. "Just have to be patient."

"Still," you say, "I'm not sure I'd have the strength to do what you do."

After work, sit in a tub full of bubbles. Stretch your neck forward, resting your forehead on the tops of your knees. Aaron washes the tension from your back, pushing suds along the lines of your torso, the curve of your waist. He tells you this isn't worth it—coming home so upset. Coming home with pains in all your bones. Not worth it.

"He's an idiot," you tell him. "I've never dealt with a director like him."

"He's frustrated. You ignore him and he lashes out. How do you feel when he calls you Asia?"

"Do I look like the continent of Asia?" you snap and seeing the worried look on Aaron's face, soften, say, "I'm too annoyed to feel anything." Tell him it won't be much longer. "We need the money."

Day Five of Nine

Today you sleep in a little. Your call time is a little later than usual, eight A.M. This is because the production is moving onto the stage. On the one hand, this is good, you start a little later. On the other hand it also means you could stay and work there till six tomorrow morning.

Drive along the lake in silence. Still sleepy, you barely notice the rush hour traffic around you. The sky is gray and you can hear the wind dash along the beach. You think you hear the waves crashing onto rocks, but you're travelling much too fast to actually hear the water. You've stopped dressing up for work—not that you ever were dressed up. You've taken to wearing old T-shirts and faded jeans. Instead of boots, wear tennis shoes that are weathered with dirt and mud. You shower but no longer blow-dry your hair or curl it. You've given up on makeup.

Driving, you wonder how long the day will be. What insults you will be subjected to today. For the past few mornings, Bud has thanked you for coming back to work, has told you how much the company appreciates your patience. Patience, my ass, you think, I can't afford not to come in. Last night your *lola* told you to sue the man. "Where we come from young ladies don't let men act this way."

"*Lola*, it's not like I'm encouraging this," you cried to her.

"Then you should speak up, *hija*, you should speak up."

Imagine telling Dick off, or walking off set for the day—or burning all your notes and quitting the job for good. That would screw him big time. No one would be able to pick up where you left off. He'd be lost. Think about turning him in, filing a suit, writing the *Chicago Tribune* or *Variety*. Imagine you and Keiko, friends, sisters, pow-wowing, letting him have a taste of his own recipe, coming up with other ways to cook sausages. You could fry them, roast them, bake them, skewer them on metal sticks, cut them up into little round pieces. You could—a taxi cuts you off and you slam on the breaks, honk the horn, you scream, "Asshole!" You hope the day is short.

Dick stands in front of a kitchen facade and stares at you as you sit on an apple-box, reviewing your notes. The page before you is sparse. You've stopped writing down the things you hear. Wonder if you're even hearing conversations at all any more. You can feel him watching you, sense him out of the corner of your eye. Finally, look up and ask, "Do you want something?"

"Nothing," Dick says, "Well, actually, tell me something, Elena."

Begin poring through your notes, looking for the answer to the question he will ask. "What were you and my wife talking about?" he asks.

"Didn't she tell you?" you say as you continue to search your notes. You see that yesterday you forgot to write down what time the camera rolled first shot. You've stopped writing down complete sentences too. Sometimes you wrote, "Good" or "Okay," sometimes "Not good."

"I guess I forgot to ask."

"Well then, I suppose you'll have to remember, won't you?" Smile at him. Challenge him.

"You know, Asia," he says, "you don't need to be so meticulous." He leans over you, casting a shadow onto the pages of your notes. He whispers into your ear, says, "I mean, it seems that you haven't caught me being untrue—not to the script."

You decide not to answer him at all. He is talking to someone in the room named Asia or Ellen and you are neither of these persons.

Because you do not answer him, he stands and strutting far from you calls out, "You know Asia, your notes are looking pretty bare—I sure hope you haven't missed anything. Could cost us a lot of money, you know. Could cost you your job."

He gets up and walks over to the clients. Unclench your hand from the pencil. You haven't even noticed how hard you've been holding on. Glancing at your notes, see the words you've written down etched deep into the page.

Watch Katy scrubbing at the O'Connor's kitchen sink. Her hair bobs frantically as she scours the sink with a shower of cleanser. "Elena," she says, "do you remember if we had the shade drawn in the wide shot last Friday, or was it up?"

Stare at the O'Connor window. Examine the light yellow drapes that hang above the sink, the little green ruffles that tie the drapery back. Imagine the wide shot in the O'Connor kitchen. You remember you shot that on day three—or was it four? Bel, alias Mrs. O'Connor, stood in front of the window and talked to

Dick's twenty-five millimeter lens. Bel had a tendency to tilt her head to the right or camera left—you can see that—and the light which hit her from the back of the facade—but you can't imagine how the window looked exactly. Did you see glass or was it that white shade? You look through the Polaroids you've taken—there aren't many. Which is unusual for you—you always take so many pictures when you're covering continuity on set.

Rifle through the Polaroids, never looking up. "I can't remember, Katy," you tell her. "I was a bit distracted."

"You're too thin-skinned, Elena. You shouldn't fight it. Play along—you'll die in this business if you don't."

"That's not true," you tell her. Continue to flip through the pictures, say, "I work with all kinds of directors—nobody in Chicago has been this rude. Makes me want to file a complaint—or write a letter to someone—I don't know. God, I could quit. Screw 'em all."

"You wouldn't do that, would you? Think of all the people you'd piss off—you'd be a wave maker. No one would hire you."

Look up from the stack you've been shuffling. Stare at Katy. Pause and then say, "Thanks, Katy, thanks for the support."

"Plus," she calls to you, "you wouldn't get paid."

When Bud calls lunch at one o'clock, everyone leaves the room except you. You run your hands along the pages of your notes searching for the words you've written—or thought you'd written. It's weird that the pages are as empty as they are, because you seem to have been writing all this down—yet none of it exists except for cursory words like "Good" and "Best" and "No Good." Standing up, you place your notes on a chair against the wall. When you turn to leave you are caught off guard by Dick who stands in front of you. He presses up against you. Pinches you between him and the studio wall. He laughs. "Do you like lunch?" he asks. "Keiko likes lunch, that's why she comes to set, for lunch."

"Let me go."

"Elena, you're not coming onto me, are you?" He smiles at you and you can see the yellow of his teeth. "I'm flattered, Elena, but I'm a happily married man, you know."

"You bastard, you wouldn't." He leans down and the breath of his words lands in little moist clumps on your nose and the brim of your lip. You can smell stale bits of nicotine and coffee. A wave of nausea rises from the knots inside you. "That's sick," you say. "You're the one." His eyes widen and you can see tiny red veins cracked in the white of his eye. Push him away.

"Name calling? Lies? Promiscuity? Careful Asia," he whispers. The weight of him against your breasts sends sharp pains through your chest. Hold still, try not to breathe his smarmy scent. His eyes penetrate your skin. "You could be fired over something like this," he says, "lose lots of work, you know?" He rubs his face against yours the way he rubbed his beard against his son's small belly that first day. He pricks you with the bristles, and you can't believe you thought he was a good father. "This," he says, "is not the kind of behavior I tolerate on sets."

The door squeaks open and Samuel comes running through. Bud follows next, chasing the child and screaming in a high falsetto voice, "I'm gonna get you!"

When Bud sees you standing with Dick flat against your chest he laughs and says, "Excuse me—I didn't mean to interrupt."

Samuel runs to his dad and Dick tells them, "That's okay. We're just coming to lunch anyway."

Keiko, trailing after Bud and Samuel, enters the room and gives you a long cold look. You push your hair out of your face, out of the corners of your mouth. She grabs onto Dick's arm and kisses him hello. They leave you standing at the wall while you wipe the sweat from your lips, your brow and forehead. You hold your hands out in front of you and watch them shake. Quickly gather your notes which have fallen from the chair you placed them on. The lines you've drawn on them are blurred. You blink tears from your eyes. The papers seem to stare at you blank as white walls. How can she put up with this, you think? How can she say nothing? Toss the papers, kick them out of your way.

Leave.

Day Six of Nine
Sleep until noon. Speak to no one, not even Aaron. Walk around the house. Start to do things. Chores. Eat. Watch TV or read a book then stop. Accomplish nothing. You're not sure what has happened, only this: You feel weird.

Day Seven of Nine
More of day six.

Day Eight of Nine
Come out of hiding. Put your arms around Aaron and hold him for almost an hour. Tell him how much you want to cry. "Go ahead," he whispers. But you shake your head and say, "Can't." Tell him it's like being in shock. Tell him you are numb—your chest, your limbs, your heart.

Go for a walk. Answer the fifteen messages on the machine. Book yourself on two jobs. One starts next week. The other starts in three weeks. Ask who's directing.

Day Nine of Nine
Sit by the window of Millie's Matzo Madness, drinking bowls of soup. Your stomach's sore. You are alone and mumbling into matzo ball broth, reading matzo dough like a gypsy reads tea leaves. Rub the palms of your hands, trace the lines that Letty said spell out your life. You're confused and don't know which lines meant long life, stubbornness or strength. Cup your hands in order to define the creases—the lines are gone. The palms are blank as white paper.

Dream about life-size erasers and gallon tanks of white-out. Wish you had some. On the napkin before you, scribble notes to yourself. You will write a letter, call a senator—maybe the one from Pennsylvania, make up a song or poem, a cautionary jingle. Warn everyone. Tomorrow you'll get tickets to Oprah's show—

you'll offer to be a guest on her program, "The Choices Women Make."

You should have gone with your gut. Quit the moment you saw it coming. Did you see it coming? Left the day Danny Boy's sausages were no longer Danny's. When filming sausage was no longer the point. Now, even though you're the one who left, it seems that he has won.

Look down the center of your body. What do you see? A pair of legs. Legs that begin just beneath your chin, stretching long and narrow like a strip of highway somewhere in the middle of desolate Nebraska. Turn your head and look out Millie's picture window. Stare at your reflection, the contours of your face, the way your cheekbones sit wide and high, cocked at angles—the way your chin draws to a point and your hair feathers and frames your face like the Pacific Ocean borders Asia. You are Asia. The continent of Asia. Asia with long highway legs and blue-black hair. You are a slender hand. A delicate foot. The curve of a woman's hip. A teacup breast. You are an entire race of women. Chinese, Japanese, Filipina, Vietnamese. Fragmented and seemingly free, you have lost your edge. Your name. The soul that you once recognized. You've lost the continuity of self.

MIX LIKE STIR FRY

Born on the very edge of the east coast of the United States of America, you've lived in many places, known your share of McDonald's and Wendy's lunches, dinners in an assortment of Chinatowns. When you were growing up, there was no place to go for Thai food, Vietnamese food, Korean or Filipino food. There was only Chinese food. And people would say, "Let's go out for Chinese," like they were out to get a China man or woman.

Later, your parents planted you in the heartland, among wheat and corn. You drenched your share of grilled cheese sandwiches with bottles of chocolate milk. You and your brothers watched *Leave It to Beaver* and *I Dream of Jeannie*, sometimes before nap time, sometimes after. At dinner you ate several dishes with rice—beef, pork, chicken—seasoned with soy sauce, not salt from the girl with the umbrella, but soy sauce from the Asian mart.

When you moved to Brookfield, kids at school assumed you were a Chink or a Nip. They did the usual tugging at the corners of their eyes, chanting, "Chinese, Japanese, dirty knees look at these." Of course, you're not sure how the rest goes, or even if this is how it went. You were too busy running away or plugging your ears, never really listening.

In high school, you worked hard to fit in, not knowing what
else to do. In a cluster of girls, you leaned against green metallic
lockers, one leg up, sinking your small chest into books and fold-
ers, trading secret-coded notes with Sarah Schaefer, Perrie Olson,
and Mary Jo Starr, giggling when the boys drifted past, always
giggling. Your favorite thing to do was to strut around in red-
tagged Levis, a faded denim shirt and clogs, a Farrah Fawcett
perm, your All-American teenage look. You could talk fast like
the best of them. So fast that you and Sarah would compete, test-
ing your endurance, speaking run-ons that went two minutes
without a breath, so fast you clipped your words, so fast you spoke
in initials. I.B.D.I. meant I don't believe it. You listened to R.E.O
Speedwagon and Foghat. Knew every single word—every
breath—to Meatloaf's "Paradise by the Dashboard Lights." You'd
grown into the typical teen. Were invited to all the senior parties
because you were "in"—one of them—a Brookfield girl, a
Wisconsin Badger, All-American, and somehow your color was
lost, bleached from your face. People said, "You're a minority?
Really? Which one?"

Shaped in such a way, you no longer stuck out, weren't
different, you laced your spoken language with "likes" and "ya
knows." You cracked gum and travelled in packs of teenagers who
spoke at once, never listening, never bothering to check your
grammar. You sat at the counters at Mac's, drinking shakes and
eating fries after football games, games you never watched, only
attended. You did good, girl. You got letters from your cousins in
the Philippines, little works of art, carved in ornate letters and
perfect English. They were not hip to your Brookfield slang.
You'd write them back with bubble-penmanship, writing that
now makes you think of comic strip dialog, just to show them
how cool you were, how great the States were, how backwards
their traditional lives must be. And still, after all that work, something was not right. You were like that piece people jammed into
thousand-piece puzzles, shoved into the corners of other perfectly fit pieces, regardless of what shape you were. Sure, you blended

in pretty well, wore the right colors, did your best to look the part, but you were part of the sleeve, the shoulder of the puzzle, and you were placed somewhere in the torso.

And after you moved to the big city, you noticed how brave strangers were, how they didn't think twice about stopping you on the street, pausing at the entrance of the subway, asking, asking, asking, "Are you Japanese? Speak Chinese? Come from Vietnam?" No. No. NO. None of your business, you'd say. Where are you from, you'd ask. Sometimes you ignored them, but more often than not, too irritated to leave it alone, you opened your mouth and the words spilled out. "Brookfield," you'd tell them with a snarl. "I'm from Brookfield, Wisconsin."

Occasionally, you'll meet an American soldier who was stationed on Clark Airforce Base near Mount Pinatubo. Before he says hello, he's smiling at you, somehow recognizing you and saying, *Ano ng pangalan mo?* What's your name. Or, *Maganda ng babae ka.* Like you'd believe any stranger who says you're a beautiful girl in English, much less *Tagalog.* You've walked out of restaurants, or parked your car downtown, and sometimes they just yell from across the street. *Maganda ng babae ka! Ganda!*

Ignore those hecklers the same way you're deaf to construction workers and frat boys. Think of those women who worked the strip in Olongapo, sliding their bodies around poles, dancing seductively for their rent, for their bastard babies, curling their tiny brown legs against the white pillar thighs of the boys from the States. Wonder why it is these soldiers talk like this, telling you you're so beautiful in a language neither one of you grew up speaking. Know what they're saying and still shake your head and say, "I'm sorry, I don't understand."

Finally, after all the voices, hear your own and know, you are one of a kind. An anomaly. Making waves is what you do best. Take everything you've been told and taught and given and heard and not heard, everything that you are and mix fast like stir fry. Go about your business, sorting laundry as you go, leafing through your bills, counting ghost crabs on the beach. This is your life. Ignore the voices who want you to explain. You don't have to. It is enough for you to know you are not white, you are not from China or Japan or even, you're not even from the Philippines, the place where your parents are from. You are from the Midwest. You are an American. You're what they call American-born-Filipina.

Some will look and not recognize you, not see the color of you, will insist, "This world is really black and white, and you are white." While others, brown as you and darker will say you're nothing without this auburn hue, you are only where you are because you were born a brown girl. They will not hear the music in your voice, see the color of your actions, know the merit of your work. Ignore them. This is your life. Get on with your day— changing lanes on east-coast highways, rubbing Buddha bellies everywhere, planting basil in milkbox gardens or cracking jokes in your sweet, sweet lover's bed. Get on with it. Look in the mirror. See. At last, your voice rises above the others and speaks to you, guides you, brings you to this place where you can find your wild American self, a woman who speaks out with nasal twang, drinks beer with brats and rice, and dances when no one's looking.

COLOPHON

The text of this book was set in Caslon type with Delphian display. It was printed on acid-free paper, and smyth sewn for durability and reading comfort.